IⅣ | Experience

Iɪᴠ | Experience

Aloha
ʻOe

J.A. Mitchell

To Cervoa,

Thanks for playing the part of muse, then, and still now. You always inspire.

Give me truths;
For I am weary of the surfaces,
And die of inanition.

-Ralph Waldo Emerson

One

He climbs the steps to the elevated train platform. He's in no particular mood today; again, the world is average and uninspiring. He contemplates basic principles of force, what interests him most about his life as a mechanical engineer.

Halfway up the steps he begins to feel uneasy. As he takes more steps, his worry grows. He begins to show complete confusion. He reaches the top of the steps and looks around, perplexed. He walks down the platform staring at people, signs, and the track. Looks, he is getting looks and he looks back intensely. He walks near the platform's edge and stops. He lowers his head, his sight reaching his shoes, and he closes his eyes. There he stands for a moment, all eyes fixed on him. Slowly, he lifts his head, opens his eyes, and stares straight ahead.

He whispers inaudible words to himself. Then a bit louder; "I don't know who I am." Again, "I don't know who I am." Louder still, "I don't know who I am." He screams in an agony of confusion, "I don't know who the fuck I am!"

From below, the clamor of heavy footsteps reaches the

1

platform. Something is coming hard and fast up the steps. Five men appear, dressed in black from head to foot. Vests and helmets with large tinted visors complete their uniforms. They all rush the engineer and try to subdue him. He fights them, pushing and shoving. Finally, they wrestle him to the ground, pinning him under the collective weight of their bodies.

"I don't know who the fuck I am," he continues to say, alternating between whispers and shouts. "How the fuck do you know who *you* are?" he questions the world, and then, looking to the man whose knee is pressed against his chest, peering beyond the tinted blackness of a visor, he asks, "Who the fuck are you?"

This officer stands, his attention still fixed on the engineer. Slowly, he looks around, and then turns around.

"Commander? Commander? You alright?" comes from the muffled voice of an officer to his right.

The commander continues staring forward, facing away from the scene. Suddenly, he turns and rushes the officer who spoke, throwing him onto the tracks while making great effort to avoid the third rail. He swings his baton at the head of another officer who tries to stand, and connects, letting out an electric shock that forces the officer back. He follows with two more blows to his head, both powerful and accurate; they crack his helmet and leave the officer bent and motionless on the ground.

The engineer looks at him in surprise. The first rays of the sun illumine and enliven the early morning spectacle while breathless onlookers watch from a distance, their curiosity bested by the violent display.

An officer at the engineer's side grabs for his baton. He

stands and steps over the engineer in an attempt to engage the rogue officer while his back is turned. Before he can reach him, the engineer grabs his ankle. The officer looks down to decipher the obstruction and before he can look up, a shoulder connects with his sternum, pushing him back. He trips over the engineer on his way to the tracks and lets out a loud wail as he lands in the tracks on his back.

The engineer, whose arms are now free, throws his body forward toward the officer who is holding his legs. The engineer connects with the officer, knocking him back toward the tracks, where he collides with an officer who's trying to climb back onto the platform and who is consequently, uncontrollably, thrown back into the tracks. His arm glances the third rail and sparks fly as electricity accelerates through his body. A fire starts on the smoking, black, charred mass left behind.

Terror, shock and disbelief paint the faces of commuters. Everyone is motionless, still, staring. The lone officer remaining slowly turns to his rogue commander. They stare at each other through black visors until the commander turns to the engineer. "Let's go," he says.

The words wake the engineer out of his daze. He gets up and they both begin to run to the edge of the platform, dodging onlookers who also try to dodge them.

"Why the hell did you help me?" the engineer asks as they run.

The rogue officer removes his helmet and throws it aside. "Because this isn't the first time this shit happened. And I've been wondering myself lately, who am I?"

Running down the stairs, trying to exit the station, the two men make their way at a fevered clip while avoiding commuters. The engineer runs behind the officer, allowing him to be their guide.

"Hey, you!" they hear when they reach the bottom of the steps. "Where do you think you're going?" The shout comes from the booth beside the turnstiles. A large man in a transit uniform stands in the doorway with a phone to his ear.

Quick glances from the runaways to the transit worker validate their aversion to the hostile voice. They both dart toward the turnstiles. The officer thrusts himself over with the use of his arms. The engineer imagines himself executing a similarly athletic move, but cannot coordinate his body for the jump. Instead, he throws his weight awkwardly into the turnstile, expecting to glide through. "Fuck!" he shouts as his leg slams into the metal pane of the electric turnstile before it can open. Despite the pain, he keeps moving.

"Where are we going?" he screams as they barrel through the station, the darkness of the underground tunnel shrouding them, providing some semblance of obscurity. They still receive stares from a few curious and confused onlookers who they actively navigate around.

"Outside—Away from here!" the officer responds.

Ahead, light emanates from a staircase into the station, and rests upon the cold, hard, grey substation floor. "There, we're going up!" the officer shouts again.

The engineer takes a right at the staircase and begins to ascend. The light streams by him as he rapidly climbs steps. He blinks rapidly, trying to focus as he watches the officer

4

quickly scale stairs by twos. He reaches the top of the staircase and finally bursts through a barred metal turnstile and onto the street, the bright light almost blinding him. Waiting for his sight to acclimate and nearly out of breath, he turns toward the officer beside him and watches him as he scans the late morning scene.

"Did you see that? He was on the goddamn phone! Did you see that? We're fucked. What's wrong with you? You're a fucking police officer! Now what're we supposed to do? They're going to come and cart us away. We won't get lucky again, we can't fight all the police in this city. I'm just a guy who was having a bad morning. Why would you—"

"Hey, hey, calm down! Are you really like this all the time? I thought you were just having a bad morning."

"No. Man, I'm sorry. I'm sorry. I'm just all mixed up."

"We really don't have time for this. We've both made a decision, even if we don't understand it right now. Are you with me or not, guy? I'm not going to be carrying around dead weight. I don't know what's going on, but there seems to be . . . something doesn't feel right, hasn't felt right for a while, and we both seem to be on the same page. I don't know you, but I could use you, at least for a sanity check. So, what is it?"

The information, the situation, thoughts begin to swirl around the engineer's head. His mind goes numb and he stares blankly at the officer who shakes his head, turns, and begins to jog away.

"Wait, man, wait! I'm with you, I'm with you!" the engineer screams as the officer turns back around. The officer stares into the sheepish engineer's eyes and sees resoluteness not present before. "You got a plan?"

"We work in units and we patrol in rotation. Every unit has at least a twenty minute response time to those adjacent, in a high traffic area like this, probably ten. So that gives us about seven minutes. Judging by the severity, or really the insanity of what we just did, we should see two units around this area within the next seven minutes. I give us about twelve to fifteen before we're staring at authority."

"So what're you thinking? You got a car or something?"

"We're on foot patrol. Patrol car's a couple stations north. Unless you think you can get a vehicle to this location within the next five minutes, I suggest we start running," the officer replies.

"Cab!" the engineer points, screams and starts whistling wildly while waving his hands in the air. A cab, which had just taken a left in their direction speeds up and stops directly in front of them. "Fucking hallelujah!" the engineer exclaims.

They walk between two parked cars and enter the cab hastily.

"Where to?" the portly cabbie asks by rote.

They stare at each other. "Uhh . . . take us to . . ." the engineer begins anxiously.

"Bishop and Merchant," the officer finishes.

"Got ya," the cabbie replies by rote.

The engineer looks at the officer who stares out his window. The engineer follows suit. They both sit back in a state of calm bewilderment, accepting the possibility that these might be their last peaceful moments.

"For fucksake, I really can't stand this, monthly fucking

protocol, unit restructuring, time suck, life suck . . . how the hell can I be responsible for everything that goes on in this . . ."

"*Captain*?" Commander Natal walks in on her obviously distressed captain and watches as he incoherently mumbles. The words seem to fuel him as he stares at the screen in front of him while striking the keyboard forcefully but efficiently. He continues to grumble for a few more seconds until he accepts the presence of another person in the room.

"U-R, I'm just complaining to the only person that'll listen. What do you need, commander?"

"Unit Restructuring? Is Director Benghazi on leave today?"

"Benghazi's been transferred."

"Transferred? Do you know where?"

"Dunno, and didn't even know about it, left like a thief in the night. We just got the paperwork today. Transfer should be here in a couple days. You got to love the timing, beginning of the month with no heads-up. Wherever it is must be having some issues, he was a darn good director." The captain finally lifts his head and folds his hands in front of him. He raises his chin, giving his full attention. "What do you need Natal?"

"Just got called in, captain, another Spook."

The captain sighs and shakes his head. "Again? It never ends, does it?" he grumbles under his breath. "Where?"

"Wiki Station. It gets worse." Natal pauses and stares intently at her captain.

"What, commander?"

"It was an officer, sir. Well a civilian and an officer."

"Tell me, commander, what happened? Just give me the info."

"Sir, a civilian appears to have undergone a mental lapse.

But, unlike most Spook events, this one turned violent. The civilian began to yell and shout uncontrollably. A unit was in the area, sir, and heard the shouts. They responded and engaged, but . . ."

"But what, commander?"

"An officer in the unit aided him and a fight ensued. Both perps were able to escape. One officer was rendered unconscious, but is now stable. Another, sir . . . another, he's dead, sir. An officer contacted the third rail of the tracks . . . and he's dead, sir."

The captain leans back in the chair. His face falls into the shadows. He rests his elbows on the arms of his chair, his fingers meet in front of him and he sits quietly. Commander Natal stands with her helmet under her armpit for several uncomfortable seconds.

"What's the situation on the ground?" he asks with a gravity that Natal feels.

"Sir, of the two officers remaining, one stayed with the injured and the other went to track the perpetrators. The station has been shut down and Municipal Transit is dealing with rerouting commuters. Emergency and Aid personnel are at the site. They're in the process of pulling the body from the tracks."

"Have the officer at the site assist directing personnel. I want you to contact the officer that's following the perps and report any progress. Whoever it is, I want the Unit Commander back here ASAP. In my office ASAP. Do you understand me, Commander?" Silence. "Commander?"

"Sir . . . the rogue officer *was* the Unit Commander, sir."

"Who? Who was the commander?"

"Commander Charles, sir."

"Mike?"

"Yes, sir."

The captain slowly leans forward in his chair, and light again illuminates his face. Entranced, he looks down. His voice levels off. "Those f-in' Spooks," he says softly. "Commander Natal, I want you to rotate out with the next commander that has house duty. I want you on this. No director, so I need you to put together a unit. I want the unit request in the system within an hour. I'll take care of it. And I want you to find Commander Jezequel and brief him on the situation. You two are point on this and you call in any help you need. I want progress reports every two hours unless you're otherwise indisposed. Natal, do you follow me?"

"Yes, sir."

"Good. I need this resolved, and I trust you to resolve it."

"Yes, sir," Natal says as she turns and exits through the double glass doors.

The brass knob turns, the door opens and the dim hallway light briefly illuminates the pitch-black enclosure. The door closes and once again darkness reigns. A figure stumbles inside the room, running its right hand along the wall until it finds what it's looking for. A switch is flicked, and Commander Natal begins to peel away layers of outerwear until she is left under the light fixture in uniform trousers and a V-neck tee.

She walks through the home, holding her recently shed layers in one arm while navigating with the small amount of light coming from the entrance hallway. She takes her first right and walks to the sofa in the small living room. Keeping the light off, she plops down and forces the furniture to absorb and cushion her full weight on impact. Her eyes close and she remains motionless, still, acclimating to her less intense surroundings. Her eyes slowly begin to open as she simultaneously grasps for the remote. She turns on the large wall screen that brightens the entire room. The aquatic channel plays, the image glides gently through the ocean, serenely capturing its grandness and beauty. Natal allows the image and the soundtrack to pervade her senses in her attempt to drown out the day's events.

So engulfed in her state of disregard and with her eyes still adjusting to the darkness after the flood of light, Natal doesn't notice the form sitting on the sofa to her left for several moments. Slowly, she begins to decipher a clear figure out of the corner of her eye. Eventually, the amorphous object begins to take the shape of a person when her sight begins to settle. With her eyes fixed ahead and with no change in her temperament, she slowly reaches for her firearm, feeling blessed that the day's exertion did not afford her the energy to put it away. With her eyes still focused on the endless ocean and her expression still vacuous, her hand reaches the weapon's handle.

"Please, relax," she hears before she snatches her pistol and aims it at the intruder.

"Put your arms up!" she screams. Two arms slowly extend outward and then calmly upward. Natal walks back to the entrance of the room, neither attention nor aim wavering, and flicks on the light switch.

"Mike? What the hell? What the hell are you doing here,

Mike!" Natal gushes the flurry of words and questions while the weapon remains poised. Charles stares back blankly. "Commander Charles, I'm asking you nicely, what the hell are you doing in my house . . . Commander?"

"I don't know," is his response. "I don't know." He lowers his arms and places his head in them, rubbing his forehead with his fingers and letting out a deep and mournful sigh.

"Commander Charles, listen to me. You're going to need to keep your hands up, and you're going to have to explain to me why you're in my home. I'm going to ask you again. Why are you in my home?"

Charles doesn't respond, and instead begins to stand.

"Mike! Listen to me. I have full authority to treat you as a hostile. No sudden movements and you have to keep your hands up." He stands, staring blankly still. "Mike, *please*, talk to me," Natal says, her voice now wavering.

"Natal . . . Gwen. I need help. Gwen, I need your help," he responds, betraying his heavy mind.

"Mike, let me take you to the hospital. I'm sure they can help y—."

"I don't need to go to the hospital," he interrupts, calmly yet defiantly.

"Mike, please, they'll help you. Whatever's going on with you, I know you can be helped. I know it's a mess, but I'm sure we can figure this out."

"Gwen, I don't need a hospital. I don't need that help. I need to figure out what's wrong with me. There's something wrong with me, with us, with *this*," he says, extending an open palm towards nowhere in particular.

"Mike, what are you talking about? If something's wrong

with you, you need help. We can get you help. Mike, if you've caught the Spooks . . ."

At this last mention, he begins to laugh. "The Spooks . . . the Spooks. What does that even mean?"

"Mike, we don't know yet, no one knows. But if you're having a mental lapse, lapses in consciousness, feelings of awkwardness, irritability, divergence from normal personality traits—"

"Vomiting, diarrhea, constipation, Gwen, please don't read me a prescription bottle. I know what the diagnosis is, but what the hell does that mean?"

"Mike, it means you might be sick and we have to get you help." He takes a step forward. "Mike!" Natal says sternly. Charles puts both hands out and walks slowly towards Natal. "If you're infected, you need quarantine, you need medicine, you need help."

"Gwen, it's me. Do I sound strange? It's me, I'm not sick," he says as he continues forward.

"Mike, there are men injured, there's a man dead. Mike, stop!" He stops about ten feet away as her shout is drowned out by the soundtrack to the ocean.

"Gwen, I just want to talk to you."

"Then talk, you have five minutes until I call this in."

"Gwen, we've both worked this job for a while, but these Spooks . . . these Spook events, they just don't add up. We see these things all the time, and we just send these people to the hospital. Most of the time the medical report reads something inane like 'stress' or 'fatigue-related' symptoms; on top of that, we're told to underreport it in order to quote unquote, mitigate social malaise. That report didn't freak you

12

out? The Ministry of Health doesn't tell us anything about this thing. Mental lapses, Island Fever, that's all they can come up with. Someone, a kid probably, calls it the Spooks. It sticks, and now we have some social phenomenon. But what the hell is it? What the hell is it, Gwen? We don't get anything."

"Mike, no one knows exactly what it is. The Ministry of Health thinks it could be a number of things. It might not even be just one thing. You know it's complicated, Mike, the way we live now; we all have to deal with it. They put out as much information as they can. Statistics, health advisories, they do the best they can for society."

"Gwen, we got called to a Spook near the edge of the city once. You know how it goes, less patrol presence on the outskirts. So we're on vehicle patrol, four of us. We picked it up on the radio and we were the closest. We get there pretty fast, and I have the guys set up a perimeter while I check out the scene. A young woman had been knocked unconscious. Apparently she was acting erratic on the street, talking to herself and pacing when a mother pushing a stroller walked by. The mother, she said she was apprehensive at first but decided to ask if she was okay. The woman . . . the suspect . . . saw the baby in the stroller and accused the mother of stealing her baby. She then assaulted the mother in an attempt to take the baby. A struggle ensued, until the suspect screamed, turned around, and ran into a wall—head first. Sprinted, the witness said she sprinted head first into a wall."

"Jesus."

"Yeah, the woman with the stroller called it in. The suspect was in pretty bad shape when I got to her and I was glad to

13

hear the ambulance, but by the time I got there she was awake. I tried talking to her, to keep her awake, you know. I asked her what happened, what was going on, all that type of stuff. You know what she told me? She told me that her head hurt a lot. That all she knew was that her name was Ioana Sunia and that she didn't know where she was or how she got there, and that she just wanted to know where her baby was. That she just wanted the pain to stop and she wanted to know where her baby was."

"So?"

"Her real name was Iulia Keil and she had no children, no spouse, no family. She was an Oceanian immigrant. She worked clerical. Later I found out she had a fall at work trying to organize some shelves. She said she'd been suffering some pretty bad headaches since."

"What's your point, Mike?"

"Gwen, she was clear. She was clear as a crystal when she spoke. She didn't sound confused, distressed, nothing. It was almost like she finally poked her head through the clouds and could see clearly. The medical report read something like 'head-trauma induced psychosis,' something like that. But, she knew, I saw in her eyes she knew what she was saying. And she wasn't the first or the last. And there are others . . . other events that make me question."

"Question what?"

"What's going on."

"What, Mike? What's going on?"

For a brief moment, a strange serenity prevails as they both try to gauge the other's thoughts. Slowly they are drawn to the weight of the gun thrust between them, the physical

14

representation of the chasm between them. "Gwen, I just want to talk to you," Charles says softly, as he reaches slowly for the weapon and attempts to step forward.

"Mike, I'm serious! Stop!" she responds as softly, but terse. She tightens her grip on the weapon and raises it slightly. He looks at her body, tense and recoiled, poised like a snake ready to strike. He sees in her both fear and caring, which seem to be at odds, but above all an unflappable sense of duty. He stops his advance, his hand lingering in the air momentarily before he brings it down to his side.

"Gwen, can't you see? She was clear," he says, almost pleading.

"Mike, you break into my home. You . . . you assaulted your own unit. There is a man dead right now—"

"I didn't mean for—"

"He's dead! Mike, he's dead because of you. There's a man dead, you break into my home and you try to convince me to listen to a woman who smashed her head into a wall. Not only are you trying to convince me that she was rational *after* smashing her head into a wall, you want me to take her ramblings and find some higher truth in them. Are you the same person I've known for all this . . . are you the same person I let into my life?"

"Gwen, I am—"

"You're not," she replies sternly, glaring straight into his eyes.

"Gwen, there are other events, other situations, you have to understand. I can't explain it to you, what I did today. I had to get free. I had to be free to find out. It's not just the Spooks. It's not just the way we live."

"Then what? What is it? Why did you choose this, Mike?" she asks, imploring, appealing, as if she hopes he has the answer that will make it all okay.

"It's me," is his somber response. "I don't know who I am anymore. I mean I know who I am, Commander Mike Charles of the Zone C Security Bureau, active duty service member of the Defense Ministry. But, I don't know anymore. Remember the dream I used to tell you about all the time? All the time, I would see her. Well it wasn't a dream, Gwen. They were like visions I had all the time, walking, eating, anything. And not just her . . . I didn't, I don't just see her. I see her a lot . . . the most . . . but it's a lot of things. People, places and things, that don't exist, not in this world at least. Visions, Gwen, like memories, they're like memories, realer than the memories I have. They feel so much realer in comparison to what I believe to be real, to all of this." She looks at him cautiously, her tension easing, but she remains alert. "It's still me, the same guy that you trusted, the same guy that you let in. Don't you have any faith left in me?" he asks.

"I did trust you, Mike. I did let you in, but you never did the same for me. Against my better judgment I cared for you, and you just kept me at a distance. I was even there for you, tried to help you when you told me you were dreaming about another woman."

"Gwen, I didn't mean it like that, it was something that bothered me."

"Mike, I saw how you looked when you told me about her, like you wanted to find her, like you needed to find out about her."

"Who's being ridiculous now? It was something that was

bothering me, something that I tried to open up to you about."

She lowers her gun to the side and again looks him straight in the eye. "Then let me ask you now, Mike; how did she make you feel?"

"This is crazy. We're talking about someone who doesn't even exist."

"No, we're talking about someone who only exists in memories that you claim to be more real than reality. Why can't you answer? Honestly, how does she make you feel?" She clenches her jaw, bracing herself for what's impending. Her long oval face is made sleeker by the tightness of her silken black hair, pulled back into a long ponytail that falls below her shoulders. The narrow slits of her eyes, which barely reveal two nebulous, dark irises, indistinguishable from her pupils, now strain, waiting to decipher the words his mouth forms, and her pale, saffron-yellow skin, is now tinged red at the cheeks.

Commander Charles lowers his head in quiet contemplation. "Gwen I had to tell you about it, about her. I thought it was only fair . . . it didn't feel right not to tell you. What did you want from me, Gwen? To ignore it? To act like it wasn't happening?" his reply comes with his head still lowered.

"I only wanted you," she says, trying to maintain her composure. Mike lifts his head, his face strained. He still tries to find the right words, but looks aware of the impossibility. "I can't help you, Mike. I have to do my job. I'm asking you to leave now, and I'm letting you know that once you do, I'm considering you a fugitive. I will find you and I will arrest you . . . Please, go."

He tries to look into her eyes but she stares past him. He

walks toward the entrance hallway; their bodies converge at the room entrance. He extends his right arm to the left side of her waist as he passes and trails his hand along her stomach as he walks out. She continues to stare forward, motionless. His shoulder brushes her face as he slowly walks into the hallway and to the door.

"You forgot proud, proud active service member of the Defense Ministry," she says when he opens the door. He lingers for a moment, and then shuts the door behind him.

With an extension of her arm, she flicks the light switch, again allowing darkness to consume the room. She watches the ocean from the far wall. Eventually, leaning against the wall, she slowly slides down. Sitting on the floor, the soundtrack to the ocean fills her head. She releases the ocean water from her mind, allowing it to stream out in a single line from each eye.

Two

"Waiting, waiting, waiting, waiting—I can't take all this waiting. I thought you had a plan?"

Charles tries to look past the foliage. He squats beside a tree, rolling up his sleeping bag. He can barely make out passersby, morning joggers and strollers who amble and bound leisurely through the city park. He can't help but think how useful these people must be, how useful everyone is. The island's historic reduction of homelessness and poverty could be directly traced to the influence of LE.

"You know, I really think you might be bipolar, guy. Half the time you're just sitting there blankly thinking about God knows what . . ."

"Math, it's math. Unlike you, God does know," the engineer replies.

"The other half you're acting nuts, antsy and irritable. And what the hell's wrong with math now? Why is it all a sudden not an interesting enough topic to be preoccupied with?"

"I'm . . . I'm sorry. I don't know what gets into me. I just get so worried, so anxious."

"And then the apologies, it's like some strange routine.

You're either the apologetic mathematician or the irritable know-it-all. I really can't figure it out," Charles says. His inability to decipher the engineer's behavior was not for lack of trying. It also wasn't an annoyance. It was actually something he was grateful for despite his outward irritability.

It was a trait the engineer could not control; a constant duality. In conversation, Charles probed for two days, only to be frustrated by the blubbering and self-deprecation, or the curtness and irreverence of the man. But, sitting up the last night, the second night they were together, he overheard the engineer babbling in his sleep, discussing names and events that appeared discordant with the life the engineer had previously described. Charles had, until this point, realized that stress and fatigue were two contributing factors to the engineer's irrationality. He watched for something more.

"You know, it's just, these two days we've been talking a lot. You know, back and forth, almost like you've been interrogating me. It's like you're keeping everything in your head. I just want to know what our next move is," the engineer says.

Charles still contemplates the homeless of the island. He thinks about every broken and disoriented face he watched on patrol, every lonely and lost soul who couldn't seem to find a place. His mind finally rests on a single image, Foot Patrol in the Panhandle. He had walked by a tall, broad, light skinned man. Unlike the majority of the homeless, this man showed no fear or anxiety due to the oncoming patrol. He stood firm, speaking to himself, repeating the same name and address. "James Taylor, 1501 Pembroke Lane." Charles witnessed the man rifle the words off repeatedly, until the man stopped and, looking deep into Charles' visor, exclaimed, "What? You don't know who you are!"

He spent an hour trying to find a 1501 Pembroke Lane in Zone C, then a James Taylor at that address, anywhere. Against his own judgment, ignoring reason, he searched maps, databases, to no avail. There was something about that man. His eyes, voice, the unwavering obsession, something Charles could not place. Charles accepted the address as a foreign one, but he could not escape the incident without a feeling of inconsonance.

"The Spooks," Charles whispers.

"What?"

"Huh . . . nothing. Alright then, today we're going north."

"Really, to the North? I—I thought we were making our way off the island. Why up North now?"

"We're going shopping."

The engineer stares quizzically at Charles for a moment before going to pack. Charles, ignoring the attention, stands and looks through the shrubbery. Ensconced in their refuge, he feels the safety and comfort of the vast city park that has sheltered them for two days slowly giving way to the uncertainty that his actions will lead him toward.

His gaze rests on one spot where he can see perfectly through the concealment of the nature surrounding them. He looks across a walkway to a pond where black swans with red bills leisurely bask in their aquatic haunt. The sun glimmers off the water and the sheen makes him squint. The radiance of the whole scene manages to fill him with hope. On the opposite end of the pond, not far from the water's edge, a colorful array of flowers attract his attention. Charles thinks about how natural they appear to be in the scene, how natural the scene appears to be. Yet he knows that it has all been planted, all planned. He wonders how comfortable the plants feel. He wonders whether they feel out of place.

"And again, we take force as acceleration times mass." It was the umpteenth time Gabriel had heard this teacher explain this equation in this fashion. "Force as acceleration times mass," as if it could be anything else. He despised this phrasing of the basic mathematical principle. Almost idiomatic, he despised her lack of reverence for this basic principle of existence because he always felt reborn at the thought or mere mention of this driving mechanism of life, force. But when she said it, this birth was always accompanied by a distinct feeling of disgust, similar to a bad aftertaste. Gabriel brooded over this and became lost in thought, until his consciousness was awakened by the scribbles in his notebook:

I try and try
And fail
I try
And succeed
Only to realize that there is only inevitability
Once life happens

Consciousness brings with it the realization of how many times he had been silently reading these words over without comprehension. He scans the rest of the page and discovers an array of symbology and wordage that betray his scatterbrain. An olive branch wraps around the right side margin and snakes its way from the top to the bottom of the page. "Veritas," and "Equitas," are written diagonally at the top right of the page with each letter practically branded with black ink in a rough, graffiti-like font, among notations like, "to the victor goes the spoilage," and "consciously I despise the unconscious." A large tree with bare branches centers the page and from its limbs sprout all manner of strange fruit, from objects to words to equations, all the way to the most abstract forms ranging from stylish to grating.

Gabriel examines his class work when the bell rings. The majority of students spring up and bolt for the door, leaving a few stragglers who meander toward the door. Even as the last students are leaving, Gabriel sits, still entranced. Slowly he gets up, closes his notebook, and begins to leave. He slows down to avoid an anticipated collision with a classmate, to her dismay. With her attempt at an intentional chance encounter failing, Alohi shakes her head and sighs as she leaves the room.

Why, springs to his mind. The question, like all questions he poses to himself, is rhetorical, and an introduction to a longer train of thought. *Why does she constantly try to meet me? Just because she likes me? The way she looks she could have anyone she wants. Why me? Because I'm different? Then is it me? Wouldn't she want anyone that's different? Should I? Would I? What's the point? If I have her or I'm with her or whatever, what's the point? We'll start something and follow it to its natural conclusion, to its end. Just another series of events. Why start at all?*

When the thoughts subside, he realizes he's out the front

door. The last five minutes were a blur of dark hallways and clusters of people whom he subconsciously but masterfully weaved through. He quickly and calmly stalks through the masses of students clustered outside. Once free, he begins to count steps on his way home. The banyan boughs and sprigs bow in the wind, inviting attention; Gabriel gives none of his own. He counts steps until his mind begins to wander, covering more ground than his feet ever could. With his head crooked slightly downward, he plods along at a healthy clip until he reaches the edge of a small lush lawn. He casually strides up the walk with key in hand and enters his home.

"Gabriel, is that you?" he hears as the door shuts behind him. Without answering, Gabriel navigates the house by instinct and leisurely walks to his room. Inside, he turns on the light to reveal a bright, spacious white room. Two rows of track lights stretching the length of the room spotlight him. He tosses his bag on his bed that lies against the far wall. It barely bounces and then settles comfortably on the edge of the bed. He takes a left and sits at his desk that occupies the middle of the wall. Three computer screens face him. He stares at the central screen while he reaches under the desk and starts the computer, all while continuing to stare, entranced by the screen as his machine boots.

"Gabe? . . . Gabe? . . . Gabriel?" Neither the words nor the several knocks on the door are enough to snap him out of his trance. "Gabriel, are you in there? Well, I heard you come in! I'm taking off, hun! I didn't have time to cook but there's some tuna in the cabinet, make yourself a sandwich. I'll be back later. I feel like I haven't seen you in forever. Are you on that computer again? Don't forget to eat."

The world outside his door blends together into a mélange of triviality as he faintly registers the sound of the front door closing. His fingers begin click-clacking away at the keyboard, subconsciously responding to a request for username and password. With a click of a button he is connected with the World Wide Web and starts searching for his address of choice; d-i-d-d-o-r-o-t-.-c-o-m, his fingers type. His middle finger stabs at the Enter button, and he is immediately bombarded with images and links. Slowly his eyes scan the list of linked information, and he peruses, stopping to ingest what peaks his interest. He continues to feed his brain this brand of junk food, vegging out on the slushee of information until he unearths a video link. Spookin' Out, it reads. Another click, and he's watching a woman sitting on a well-groomed lawn in her bathrobe. Her palms rest on her scalp while she shakes her head feverishly and stares downward at the green grass. A group of young voices heard in the background provides context to the shaky camera work.

"Look at this crazy, look y'all. I told you my neighbor was a crazy," a young female voice says.

"I think she got the Spooks," a male replies.

"She got the Spooks, oooooooooohhhh." The ghastly comment comes from another teen male and produces laughter and cackles.

Suddenly, the woman's head snaps up and her eyes follow the laughter. She glares intensely into the camera shot, her whole face contorted and distressed. A distinct and unmistakable look of misery is present on her face, a look that chills Gabriel to his core. She again begins to shake her head wildly from left to right, until she stops, looks up to the sky, and

25

lets out a hellish scream that echoes inside Gabriel's gut.

"Aye, yo, turn that off man. Turn that off!" is heard over the video, which bounces about wildly until it cuts to black.

Gabriel leans back in his chair, expressionless. He glances again at the video's title, "Spookin Out," then back at the black screen. He can only see his own image reflected in darkness.

Three

"No, captain, no sign of them, we've completely lost track . . . Nope, no use of any bank accounts after they cleared them out two days ago . . . The cabby was no help, he could only direct us to the corner and we already have the bank records from the ATM they used. We have every unit scouting in the city while on patrol, we've just been rotating the same hotspots, but there's a lot of camp ground and we need more info to search effectively . . . Well, I think at this point I'm assuming they're trying to leave the Island, sir. As you know, the Coast Guard has been alerted, but I have a hunch. I really don't want to leave this area, sir . . . Alright, sir, give me twenty-four more hours and we'll leave." Commander Natal manages this whole conversation with barely a breath. She inhales quickly, bracing herself.

"Sir, permission to speak openly."

"Yes?" the captain responds in his husky voice.

"There was no mention of a mental lapse in the report, no Spooks. I saw the footage, sir—"

"Yes, you've seen it because there's a lot of trust in you, Natal, that's why you're point on this," he interjects.

"Well, thank you, sir, thank you for the trust," Natal says in her most reassuring tone, "but I definitely think there was more to that than 'an officer aiding a suspect resisting arrest,' as the report read. And the new charges of espionage, computer crimes, terrorism, et cetera. Between you and me, it doesn't sound like Commander Charles, sir."

"He is no longer a commander on this force," the captain replies emphatically. "Don't let personal attachments get in the way of work, commander. He's been investigated, Natal, and there are things about Mike that you don't know—that I didn't know. You're the woman I picked for this job. I have to be able to trust you to get it done. Can I trust you, Natal?"

"Yes, sir."

"Good."

Natal wastes no time. With the click of the line, she is immersed in the present.

"Unit One to Unit Two, Over," she relays.

"Unit Two, Come In," comes from the clear line of the radio.

"Unit Two Report Status," Natal commands.

"Unit Two on patrol in West Wing of Level 2, Over," the same determined voice responds.

"Unit Two to receive new orders. Unit Two to regroup with Unit One at the main entrance. Unit Two command will be briefed on arrival, Over," Natal orders.

"Roger, Wilco," is the response.

"Out," Commander Jezequel hears. Having received his new orders, he motions to his to troop to move out. As they walk, their sleek black uniforms meld in with the natural contradictions presented by the outdoor mall. Palm trees lined in a row through the center of the mall, and walled off by four

28

feet of slate, tower over consumers. A central waterfall can be heard throughout the entire expanse as it threatens to carry everything away in its deluge. The occasional pond subtly accentuates the scene, carrying various colorful, tropical fish. Shops line the entire structure. Thick throngs of shoppers enjoy the scenery while they browse the storefronts, looking to be ensnared by an enticing shop name or a tantalizing display, and the open air acts as the roof, offering the cover and security of the infinite sky.

The troop files along, two rows of officers walking in pairs behind Lieutenant and Commander. Tiny droplets of rain descend. Along their route, a pet shop offers a rack of perched parrots, unattended and squawking for onlookers' amusement.

"Can you believe this place? *Man*," an officer says, quietly expressing his astoundment to his cohort.

"It's the largest open-air mall in the world," his partner responds. "What do you expect?"

"Shit, this island already had the largest, now they have the first and second. What's the point? They must really not like competition," he says.

"What's the point to anything? Besides, LE wasn't here when the first one was built. They're probably just trying to prove something."

"Or compensate for something. That CEO of theirs must be short, and I don't think it's height if you know what I mean," the officer concludes.

The tiny bit of laughter solicited from the officer's partner incites Commander Jezequel to point to his ear, signaling quiet. The lieutenant relays the command and the two junior officers immediately comply.

They walk along, quiet and brisk, while shoppers hustle to avoid their path or attention. Overhead, the heavy chant of an assemblage of men can be heard, part of the hula kuhiko, one of innumerable performances of the day. ". . . latest in electronics to the most comfortable in home furnishings, LE is there when you need us," comes blaring from an advertisement on the wall as they pass. Transitory images flash rapidly on the wall projection; a woman playing with her dog in a field of grass follows a man soldering a circuit board and is succeeded by a sprinter with an artificial leg crossing a finish line. ". . . because to live is to experience. LE, Live Experience," are the words that accompany the final images as the projection fades, only to start again.

They continue past this one of numerous advertisements they've been subject to while on duty, and make it to the elevators. The elevator takes them to the first floor, where they imitate their commander's pace and slowly jaunt to the main entrance of the mall and find their counterpart company and commander positioned at both sides of the entrance.

Jezequel slowly approaches, taking off his helmet in the process. His hair is cropped short, and coupled with his pronounced forehead, makes him appear doggedly present. His long body sways slightly as he saunters to his destination, and is complemented by his long face that displays nobility and self-assurance that border on arrogance. The tension in his perpetually clenched jaw is finally released as he nears the others, unhinging in anticipation of speech.

"Orders, commander," he states, standing next to Natal.

His words are accompanied by an intimate and intense

stare that is all too familiar. She doesn't look at him; instead, she remains focused on the entryway.

"It's going to rain soon. I'm taking two officers and joining the others in the Surveillance Room. We're going to need the extra eyes. We'll monitor from there. I need you to assume command of the units on the ground and cover all entryways. No more patrols; I need you to stand guard. Coordinate with Mall Security, they're under your charge now. Understood, commander?"

"Orders received, commander," Jezequel responds.

She walks away. With each step, she feels his eyes stalking.

"You'll be fine. It's going to be raining all day, just wear the poncho with the hood and be calm, and everything will be alright."

"But if they catch me on video—"

"Look, guy, I've listened to you for half an hour talk about everything from camera angles to vectors to the probability of evading police by moped based on vehicle speed and maneuverability. I really can't take it anymore. You're going to buy light supplies at the local store. Just go in, buy them, and leave. Wear the friggin' poncho with the hood and you'll be fine. We've almost made it to the mopeds, what is it? You going or not?" Charles asks firmly.

"Alright, alright, I'm sorry. I'll go. I just don't know what gets into me," the engineer replies earnestly, "but you don't always have to be the tough guy, you know. Sometimes I feel like tagging you on the chin just to test it out. I'll go, but you don't

31

always have to fuckin' yell, you know," he finishes combatively, and with an attitude Charles is now used to seeing sporadically.

"What did you say?" Charles asks as they exit the trailhead.

"Oh, no, nothing. I'm sorry. I told you I don't know what gets into me. I think I'm just tired and a bit nervous, well—scared. But I'll go, don't worry," the engineer replies sheepishly. Motionless, Charles continues to stare at the engineer, a man of average build and simple features, and finds nothing distinguishable about him except for his constantly imploring eyes and their flashes of wildness. "I'm sorry, I'm sorry! I told you I didn't mean it. I'm all off lately," the engineer offers in his self-deprecating tone.

Charles walks away slowly, again contemplating the strange personality shift in the engineer. The rain barrels down, smacking against their ponchos. Charles walks along the highway, followed by the engineer, until they duck into the woods. Weaving through the trees, they travel a short distance until they come to a rock face with leaves piled high in front of it. They both begin to diligently brush away the leaves, excavating two mopeds, one grey, and the other black.

"So are you going to at least tell me where you're going?" the engineer asks in his sheepish tone, cautious not to offend.

"Rich, I just have some things I have to take care of. I'll be back at the campsite tonight. If you get those supplies, we'll be good for the next couple days. Just trust me, I'll be back," Charles reassures as they walk their mopeds the short distance back to the road.

"Alright, to Hale'ewa!" the engineer declares, as he turns

the ignition.

"Back here tonight," Charles shouts as he starts his bike. With the road clear, they ride off in opposite directions.

Commander Natal sits, intently watching the screens before her. Through her peripheral vision she can make out her subordinate glaring at her. She ignores the instinct to reprimand him and instead reserves her energy to focus. The stale air in the surveillance room scented by the odor of burnt coffee serves only to sharpen her acuity.

She watches wet shoppers covered in rain gear amble from shop to shop. A young girl in a rain jacket tramples about in a small puddle. The splashes created by the child's militant stomps distract Natal as she becomes entranced by the child's fervor.

"What a day for this, huh," she thinks out loud. "I'm going to need you to redirect all cameras directed at crowds. I want you to bring up all five electronics stores in the mall. I want every access point and computer department covered."

"Sure thing," replies the technician.

"And I need you to try to look beyond the outerwear. He's 5'10, 210 pounds, dark skinned. Some of you know him personally, and you've all been briefed. Check the walk, mannerisms, let me know what you find."

Natal settles back in her chair, prepared for the long haul. Her eyes flutter as they move from screen to screen. Time passes at its natural pace, uncontrollably, as she wonders about the nature of the case.

"Ma'am?" The somewhat reticent voice snaps her out of

her focused trance. "Third screen down from the left. I think I spot the mark: green poncho browsing for laptops."

Natal turns to the screen and sees a man casually sauntering about. At first sight, he fits the description. His long poncho covers most of his body and a hood covers his face, but even so, she can see a stark difference in gait. She watches him walk, observing how he slightly favors his left foot, pushing off sturdily with the right and planting with a subtle limp on the left, allowing the leg to uncomfortably absorb the weight of his body until the right, reassuringly, once again takes responsibility for balance and ambulation. The man's body sinks a bit instead of expanding to the full volume of his frame, and he appears to be carrying about ten extra pounds. All of these barely perceptible traits become glaring incongruities to Natal. Her mind begins to spin. *Is he that good?* She thinks. *Did he get hurt in the subway? It didn't show in the footage. After?*

"Ma'am, how should we proceed?" questions an overeager voice coming from the farthest corner of the room. She quickly weighs her options as the man walks to the checkout with a new laptop in tote. She opens her mouth to speak once he reaches the counter, but is interrupted when the man takes off his hood.

With his side turned to the camera and his face covered by a taller customer, she watches a verbal interaction between customer and clerk, waiting for an image that will relieve her of the responsibility of conjecture.

"Do you have any camera directed—"

"No, ma'am," responds the technician, "every angle isn't perfect. Tricky spot; this is all we got," he elaborates.

"Couldn't script this better in the movies," Natal exhales, as the man turns his back to the camera and begins to leave the store. "Radio Commander Jezequel," she orders, "give him a location—" She stops. The man, intrigued by some device at the store's entrance stops and turns, which gives Natal an open look at his profile.

Mike? The mental outburst was so loud that she can't tell whether it was also verbal. Just as quickly as Charles' image appeared, it fades into a man with a stubbier face and broader features. "Disregard previous orders," she commands while glancing around. Nothing but intent and receptive faces put her at ease. Disturbed by the momentary trick of mind, she recedes into her chair and once again focuses on the screens before her.

Her mind settles again as she once more begins to lose seconds. Even under her present circumstance she appears radiant. Her silken black hair is, as usual, wrapped into a tight bun that elongates her already slim, elegant face. The yellow tint to her smooth skin appears golden and her cheeks and lips are rosy. The darkness of her garb only brings out her radiance so that even uniformed she is a constant distraction, especially to her fellow officers who sneak glances now from impulse rather than reverence.

She receives all the attention with stoicism. Too perceptive and intelligent to be unaware or bothered, she remains focused while quietly pondering her current circumstance.

The nature of the case dogs her; a media blackout of the event, no images given to the public for identification, even the Department Briefing only listing the other offenses. *Everything that came after*, she thinks to herself. It was definitely easier to stomach. Most people knew Charles was training to succeed as Administrator of Computer Systems; a desk job she knew he coveted. The desk job she also coveted, the job she hoped would allay their fears of taking the next step. *I'll quit for him,* she would think to herself. *No more danger, no more sneaking, nothing to keep us apart. We'll settle,* was her hope.

Why, is what she cannot be reconciled with. Why the need to obscure reality? That question, which she had previously been successful at ignoring, the question her focus was able to push aside, was now all she could contemplate. It was now in direct conflict with her resolute dedication to her work. But with the thought firmly planted, the roots now begin to grow. *Things she doesn't know,* she recalls the Chief saying. *Things I don't know,* she continues, and while contemplating the unknown she cannot help but think about the converse. *Who does know?* And with that question, uncomfortable thoughts begin to pour into her head.

Chief, Commissioner, Ministry—the filters of knowledge begin to frame a complex reality she had long been successful at avoiding. These thoughts that she can no longer suppress surface and produce turbulent waves in her mind. For so long she had operated with a blanket sense of trust in those above her, not out of ignorance but what she now realizes was comfort. With her comfort now shattered, all that remain are questions; uncomfortable questions she is unsure whether she wants answered.

The torrent of thought is inescapable and only leads back to him. *Why? Did he do it? Did he disregard her? Is she not as good as an image? Did he throw it all away, did he throw them away?* And then she is in her bed, with him. The sheets feel good on her naked body, caressing her as she furtively rubs her legs against the red silk. His body cuddled behind her is a reassuring presence that she fights not to touch, allowing him to rest. His arms engulf her, and she lies blissfully examining his left hand. She thinks it is the part of his body with the most character. His pinky and ring finger are a bit enlarged from over-healed fractures. A long scar outlines the outside of the hand. A dark circle in the middle of the hand reminds her to discover whether it was a cut or burn. She stops at the mark, transfixed. She is completely captivated and watches as the hand begins to move away, the arm becomes more and more distant until the hand and its mark are attached to an arm, and then a man wearing a black poncho. The man walks and as his arm sways, the dark center of his hand is the only distinguishing mark she can see and is barely perceptible when in view. Natal realizes she is watching a screen in the Surveillance Room.

"Ma'am—"

"Radio Commander Jezequel," she interjects. "Let him know the mark has been spotted on the Third Floor, West Wing, LE Computing Center. I'll reassume command of all other personnel, I need his unit in pursuit," she says, as she watches Charles in a black poncho, walk into the LE computing center and set up shop at one of the stations on the long table against the wall. 'Did I, could I really have seen that on his hand?' she thinks.

She watches Charles working intently on the computer. His fingers move rapidly at the workstation. His dark skin practically shines as the fluorescent lighting bounces off his hands and face. "I need you two here," she says as she

37

stands and points to two officers on the Surveillance Team. "Survey the suspect and update me. The rest of you are with me. Group up!" she commands. They immediately comply, hustling up and into pairs behind their commander.

"Security Bureau Command in, Over" she says into her radio.

"Security Chief, Come In."

"The mark has been spotted. We need a perimeter lockdown. No one enters, no one exits. I need Security in the Live Experience Computing Center on standby. Do you Copy?"

"Copy. I don't know how he got in; I'm sure our men—"

"Don't worry about it," she interjects. "Were the orders received? Over."

"Received, ma'am."

"Out," she concludes. "Move out!" The troop bolts through the door.

Charles works diligently. Windows pop up and close rapidly as he surfs the web. He researches intensely, from diving points to transit routes. In between, he briefly examines a topographic map of the island. Finally he pulls up an email account and reads a message from an address identified only as Todd. "Need help, need to be free," is the text of the email which bears no subject that he sends back. He quickly unregisters the email account, deletes his browsing history and closes all windows. He pulls the poncho hood over his head and proceeds to exit the store just as calmly as he came.

On his way out, he notices store security converging, creating a bottleneck at the entrance. He feels a hand grab his shoulder. He rushes forward. Three guards reach for him and are left grasping at air as he breaks through the arm tackles. Outside the store, he barely manages to keep his footing on the stone walk as he slides on his heels. To his left he makes out a police unit racing after him. He swivels, turning to his right, and sprints down the mall corridor.

"Attention shoppers. Due to an emergency, the mall is currently being evacuated. Please file orderly and quickly to the nearest exit. Personnel are on hand to direct and assist you," is the looped message heard throughout the mall.

The thud of Charles' hiking boots colliding with the stone walk alerts shoppers of the impending trouble. They try to create a lane for him, attempting to create distance from the large foreign mass that threatens to crash into them. He weaves and pushes his way through the traffic and chaos. A leg pokes out in front of him and he slams into it, tripping. He stumbles, but regains his balance. Charles peaks back and sees a man on the floor clutching his leg in pain. "Always a hero," he mumbles as he flies down the walk, towing his weight as efficiently as he can until he sees a gang of mall security up ahead.

"Mike Charles! Do not resist, we're here to take you into custody!" Charles hears behind him. He recognizes the familiar voice, stops, turns and sees the lanky Jezequel giving chase, his stride reminiscent of a Doberman. Charles could envision his stare through the visor, that calculating glare that never subsided. Whenever their line of sight crossed, it had felt like an unconscious, silent, duel.

Charles stands at a crossroads. To his right, Mall Security waits, and to his left, Security Bureau approaches. Before him is another walkway that also extends behind him. The usually busy mall intersection is now empty save for the few dawdlers that rush to safety. He can smell the pretzels from the abandoned kiosk to his left along the curved glass panels that acts as a boundary. The rush of water coming from the waterfall beside Mall Security crowds his mind as he contemplates his options, east or west to confrontation or north or south to brief reprieve.

Confrontation is inevitable, he realizes, as he rushes the Mall Security Guards. Three local guards dressed in beige linen uniforms and armed only with batons stand in a single row and look uneasy as Charles buries his shoulder into the gut of a guard who's unable to respond in time. Another guard swings his baton with all his might—a blow that Charles is barely able to avoid by throwing his head back. After the narrow escape, Charles lunges his head forward and catches the Hawaiian's jaw and mouth with the crown of his skull, leaving the monumental man bent over. A heavy blow from the third guard lands squarely on Charles' right shoulder before he can regain composure. Charles clenches his teeth in pain and tries to lift his arm, anticipating another blow. Only pain is transmitted and again the rush of water from the waterfall, now right beside him, crowds his mind, aiding his pain but adding to his present delirium.

Charles turns and grabs onto the large guard, who remains bent and holding his mouth, before receiving a blow to his back which jostles him and momentarily thrusts him toward the direction he intended on. He bears down and drives forward, providing the momentum that carries him and the guard over the ledge of the walk and onto the rock formation that tops the waterfall. The two roll down, tussling a bit, before entering the torrent of water that carries them both down to the shallow pool below.

Jezequel finally reaches the spot of the altercation and looks down to see the guard, with blood trickling down his busted face, wincing in pain while he tries to stay afloat in the ten-foot pool. Charles rolls over the edge of the waterfall and onto the stone floor while small groups of captivated bystanders watch, then bursts through the crowd clutching his left arm. Before Jezequel can take proper aim, Charles darts outside of his sight to the left of the waterfall.

Jezequel reaches for his radio while scanning the scene but stops, momentarily engrossed by a situation to his left. Standing by the brim of the waterfall, a father clutches his wife's hands and gently consoles her while she genuflects before the pool with her head held to the sky. Jezequel can barely hear the soft pleading of her small son as he tugs on his mother's dress. "Ma . . . are you alright?" Tears stream down his mother's face as she quietly mumbles to herself. Jezequel struggles to read lips as he peers at the woman's rapidly moving mouth. Clasping her arms in his hands, her husband gives her a gentle shake. "Honey," he barely utters before his wife, in a state of hysterical ecstasy, bellows, "Lord, I am lost and confused, please deliver me. I have forsaken my vows, have mercy. Forgive me, for I have sinned!" She draws the attention of the remaining shoppers from the pleasant female voice that still calmly and politely attempts to herd them out of the mall.

With her head slanted and cocked upward to the night sky, she begins to sing, "Ag-nus De-i, qui tol-lis pe-cca-ta mun-di,

41

mi-se-re-re no-bis. Ag-nus De-i, qui tol-lis . . ."

The strength and beauty of her cadence resonates throughout the mall, snapping the patrons back into the chaotic reality. Once again, they begin to exit the shopping center, however possible. Jezequel turns to the two security guards next to him. "Please. Get that spooky bitch out of here!" he commands. Two heads nod and the two men take off. Jezequel grabs his radio and puts it to mouth, "Unit Two to Unit One, Over," he starts, as he speaks over the commotion.

". . . mall is currently being evacuated. Please file orderly and quickly to . . ."

". . . qui tol-lis pe-cca-ta mun-di, do-na no-bis pa-cem."

Four

"Mike Charles, come out with your hands up! Do not resist arrest!" Natal's booming voice elevates and dissipates in the evening sky. "Is the mark still pinned? Over."

"Yes, ma'am, we have him clearly on surveillance. He's taking the elevator to the third floor now, Over."

"Keep eyes on him, keep me updated, Out." Natal briefly switches channels. "This is Commander Natal, Over." Looking up, she catches Jezequel making his way toward her.

"Mall Security, Come In."

"We have the mark pinned, Triag, the department store. We need you to continue to redirect your men out of the Mall. No more incidents. We need the entire perimeter covered; no one gets out without being screened. Do you Copy?"

"Yes, ma'am. Sorry for—."

"No time. Make it happen. Out."

She lifts her head and feels comfort meeting Jezequel's helmet, not his face. "Confirmed, he's still in here. I've got eyes on him," she relays. "You four," she commands as she points to the trailing duo in both troops, "cover the entrance. Anything that attempts to leave here that does not wear this uniform will be detained; we don't know what can be contact. Do you understand?" A harmonious, "Yes, ma'am," follows the order.

"Both of us are going in," she says turning to Jezequel. "You trail, provide cover. Backup is on the way, should be hearing sirens soon. Locate, surround, and detain. No one engages without my order. You see him, you holler," she says brusquely, curt enough for all to digest. "Stay alert."

Natal turns and readies her firearm, simultaneously giving the order to move out.

The security screen's crisp image now captures Charles as he throws a mannequin from a large decorative orb it was expertly perched on. His actions are even more pronounced as they are broadcast on nearly every screen in the Security Room.

He proceeds to pick up the sphere. From his strain, it appears significant in weight. He heaves the largish orb as fluidly as possible at the clear pane before him that stretches the length of this section of the store, immediately clutching his left arm once it's released. The entire pane shudders, but the ball slams onto the carpet with no clear damage done to it. Charles walks away from his attempted release of frustration unsurprised, turning and kicking a rack of women's blouses, toppling it.

"Mike Charles, come out with your hands up! Do not resist arrest!" he hears from a familiar voice, and immediately begins to book it through the large department store toward the escalator and the floor above.

He ascends in leaps of twos and steps off the escalator with his arm almost dangling from his shoulder. He scours the perimeter of the floor as he did previously, only to find the same patrolled entrances with Mall Security staring at him, patiently observing and relating his actions via radio.

"These motherfuckers," he vents after he catches a guard smiling at him. Again, he begins to circle, searching for escape, until he spots a female form ascending toward him, running up the escalator with firearm poised. Charles sprints toward the exit, noticing the glowering expression of the guard switch to disorientation.

"Charles, stop!" he hears before he barges through the door that smacks into the formerly smiling guard, who is caught trying to bar the exit with his body. Charles thrusts his shoulder into the entryway again and charges through. An overeager guard to his left immediately swings low and wildly at Charles' knee, a blow he oversteps. He runs immediately for the edge of the third-story outdoor walk and scales the edge. He leaps down to the adjacent parking lot just as two shots ring out.

His legs slam into the concrete, his body the rail, with his chin narrowly escaping the same fate. Dangling from his armpits, he manages the pain silently and climbs up and over onto the cold concrete. Taking a deep breath before forcing himself up, he dashes madly through the deserted parking complex and down the ramp one level.

He comes to the edge of the building and peers over. The deserted walk is occupied by one pedestrian, who intently watches the commotion ahead. Charles rolls over the rail, and hangs off. With his arm unable to hold weight for long, he lets go, falling to the ground below abrasively. He crumples to the floor and lands forcefully on his back, looking up past the seven stories of the Mall to the darkening, colorful, evening sky as the rain pelts him.

"What the hell are you shooting at!" Natal screams at Jezequel.

"I had no shot, just trying to startle him," he responds without inflection.

"Startle him into what, leaping to death?" she asks. She shakes her head vigorously and peers over the edge of the building once more before heading back into the Mall, leaving her unit to scramble after.

"Suspect has breached exterior," she yells into her radio. "Need all units to redirect to the East side of the building. I need coverage of the parking structure and beyond." The sounds of approaching sirens offer little solace. "Suspect is on foot, he can't get far."

She tears through the store, then through the Mall past several long lines of shoppers, and bursts out the exit where she meets up with the head of Mall Security. "Is security still checking vehicles as they exit?" She asks immediately, trying to look through the heavy rain and darkness.

"Yes, ma'am, only people that were already in the lot, no one else is being allowed in." Sirens and lights fill the air as the buzz of Bureau vehicles is heard in the distance.

"And the evacuation?"

"All entryways are secure, all mall traffic is being escorted to exit points . . ." His voice trails off as Natal ingests his words subconsciously. She looks to her right and sees shoppers boarding buses, then looks ahead into the public park, trying to scan beyond the darkness. ". . . where IDs are being checked. We've called in trolley and bus support, every bus is being filled to—".

"Support? Where does regular service resume?"

"Excuse me, ma—"

"Where is the first stop after they leave the mall?" she asks, still scanning. To her left she glimpses a figure which emerges twenty to thirty yards down on the opposite walk. Tracing her sight back, she catches a trolley nearly at the stop.

"Service is running as usual, the first . . ."

Natal is gone, striding into the street, leaving him to watch as she careens through oncoming traffic with her men again giving chase. The bus stops as Natal makes it to the median of the busy road and she bolts across the other half. She reaches the sidewalk as the bus starts up again, and sees no one standing at the stop.

She gives chase, staring down the light. Sirens sound off at a distressing distance as she thinks about every stop between her and her backup. Yellow light, the bus speeds up, then begins to slow. Red light. She sprints, trying to make up the yardage.

She boards the bus with her badge out. "Police, please stay calm," she projects as she cocks her firearm. She slowly walks down the aisle until one rider goes for a window from his aisle seat.

"Mike—I *will* shoot!" With his head breaching the bus and his leg on the window ledge, he freezes. "Keep your hands up and step into the aisle," she demands, and the suspect obeys. Her backup finally boards the bus. "Remove the hood slowly." The suspect slowly removes his hood to reveal an expressionless Mike Charles. "Turn around slowly and put your hands behind your back," she orders.

47

Gabriel walks alone in his usual gait. His long legs extend before him. With each step, he meets the ground firmly and deliberately, and pushes off tersely. Anxiety permeates his aura, making those around him tense as he passes. His caramel skin bakes an even brown under the tropic sun.

"Where ya' goin'?" Alohi flanks him from the rear, her body bouncing as she walks.

He looks at her for an overextended period of time, making her question whether he'll answer.

"Ya' don have ta' be a jerk."

"To the skate park." The answer finally materializes.

"I see you holding your skateboard, why aren't you riding it?"

Another long period of silence follows the question as they both continue to walk over the short bridge that leads over the highway.

"I like the walk," he replies at his own pace. She looks at him questioningly. They walk quietly, calmly. She slowly stretches her hand out and places it under his, which tenses at the touch. She clasps his hand in hers.

At the end of the bridge, they take a right and walk together through the Makiki field parking lot toward the skate park that extends from under the bridge to the edge of the basketball court. The small skate park is teeming with local youth. Gabriel gently squeezes Alohi's hand and breaks free. Throwing his board down, he hops on and glides into the park, pop-shoving and stopping at the bowl's edge beside a cohort who watches intently.

"Aye, Gabriel, you got a new guhl, yeah?" the boy exclaims with a sly smirk.

Gabriel smiles, then dips into the bowl, sailing through and bursting into the air. Alohi watches Gabriel perform. He dips back in and flies out into an effortless finger flip before diving back into the bowl. With momentum gained, he comes out again into an early grab. He rotates 180 degrees, then flies back in at full speed. Only two other skaters venture into the bowl with him; the rest become spectators.

Shaded by the bridge, some get reprieve from the intensity of the scorching sun, but all are victims of the humidity. He skates fervently for fifteen minutes then tops the bowl suddenly. Riding to a rail, he hurtles himself up with his front foot and slides along it with the nose of his skateboard. He pops the board up into his hands and heads for the entrance of the lot, slowing for Alohi, who follows. Walking again, calmly, quietly, they both feel at ease.

"Where you headed?"

"Gotta go home, got some stuff to do," he responds.

"If I'ma be your girl, you gotta take me out, yeah?" she says, sprinkling in an accent.

"Alright."

She can't suppress a slight grin. "Friday at 9? I meet you Ward Center then?"

"Okay." She wraps her arms around his waist quickly, momentarily holding the embrace, and then walks away.

He watches her briefly, and then begins again to count his steps while he ventures home. He had the exact number from when he left that morning.

Five

Unable to sleep, the engineer stays up for the second night in a row. Anxious and uneasy, he worries about his fate and the whereabouts of his companion. There is a rustling of leaves and twigs; he believes he hears the earth being trampled. He can hear someone treading, hiking, and immediately becomes apprehensive. Tightly tucked in his sleeping bag inside the tent that now feels like inadequate security, he tries to reassure himself that this nighttime hiker is unrelated to him. With every quiet but discernible step, the unwanted intruder to his blissful mountain solitude gets closer. Knowing that he is well off the beaten path, he begins to comprehend that at this time of night this mystery hiker is coming towards him, coming for him.

He tries to invoke every spirit possible, from saint to soldier. He attempts to conjure enough bravery to move, just move. He rolls out of the sleeping bag and retrieves the firearm that Charles left behind. He brazenly opens the tent and comes face to face with his intruder.

At this point the hallucination ends, his imagination spent, leaving him firmly nestled in his sleeping bag. Now intensely timorous, tense and practically shrinking into himself, he invokes angels and demons alike for safety. He opens his eyes when he hears the tent begin to open, only to see Charles' head poke through.

"Where you been, man? I—"

"I'll tell you in the morning. We're out of here before daybreak. Get some rest," Charles enters the tent and closes it behind him. He immediately burrows into his sleeping bag, and within moments he is out.

Having passed out mid-day from exhaustion only to wake up a short time later from worry, the engineer feels sleep to be an impossibility. With nothing else to do, he closes his eyes in anticipation of a long, restless night. But with Charles sleeping quietly beside him, and an authentic sense of security again present, the engineer is out within minutes. . . .

. . . "How's your night going? Is your room comfortable?"

"It's great, reminiscent of a Hilton Village. Ever thought of room service? I think you'd make a killing. I doubt anyone's planning to go out tonight."

"You know, I'd like to think a holding cell is a great place for a bit of reflection, maybe a time for people to contemplate where they erred in judgment," Natal baits, while thumbing through the file before her.

"Definitely, a great place to spend your free time."

"Free time? I'm not sure how much of that you'll be having in the future, Mr. Charles. Who did you make contact with at the mall?"

The bright, tiny room is unalarming in a disorienting way.

51

Four bare white walls pen in a medium sized table, two chairs and the two occupants who now sit across from each other, both feeling chimeric sweat beads on their face from heat much more imagined than real. The singular, seemingly trillion watt halogen positioned above them produces a brilliant and oppressive light, which bounces off the achromatic walls, accentuating the disorientation that the environment promotes.

"I think you got the wrong guy, I don't even know why I'm here. I was just shopping and now—"

"Mike! Mr. Charles," she corrects as her tone settles. "You're facing first-degree manslaughter, assault and battery, computer crimes including cyber terrorism, actual terrorism, espionage, financial theft, fraud, evading arrest—just to name a few. At no point will you take this seriously?" she asks, closing the file.

"Sounds like an impressive resume."

"I really don't have time for this. A transfer unit from the Ministry Bureau will be here shortly, Mike. Blue Jackets are on their way. I can't help you anymore, and honestly, I wouldn't want to." She stands. "Oh, and I thought you should know. That fall, the one you walked away from with a shoulder sprain? The guard you landed on sustained multiple fractures to his leg. Lucky, really; if that water was any shallower, who knows?" She looks him down and then up, into his defiant eyes, where she notices their diminished luster replaced by something dark, something she can't identify. "You're not remotely the person I knew," Natal adds with her face twisted in disgust. She turns to leave.

"Did you really think I didn't intend to see this through, Gwen? That I won't?"

She turns back sharply, her blazing stare attempting to cut through Charles, who remains, at least visibly, unfazed. "*See what? Do you know where you are?* The Bureau Director will be here himself to oversee your transfer. You're not moving from this room until he gets here. There's just not much of a view."

The finality of Natal's statement is punctuated by the door, which slams behind her. Outside the room, she pauses in the doorjamb to quell the emotions that continue to rise.

Charles remains seated inside the luminous room. His hands, bound by handcuffs, lie on the table in two relaxed fists. He lowers his head, his eyes meet his lap and he closes them, trying to suppress the fulgency of his surroundings. In this darkness he finds tranquility, and in this tranquility, she comes. She's running away from him, playfully, and he feels himself chase leisurely, transfixed by her full, black hair, that bounces behind her. He follows until she turns her head. Her dark olive skin is flawless, and her slender face and sharp features are softened by a rounded chin. Her eyes, shrouded by full lashes, are mysterious. Her smile stalls him. He watches her run as darkness engulfs her, and is left, as always, re-imagining every detail of her.

Natal walks in on the chief while he's on the phone. Even as she stands feet from his desk, his grumbles are barely audible. One raised finger puts her on hold.

"Take a seat, Gwendolyn," the chief says, hanging up.

She assents. "I just came from the Interrogation Room. I was told you wanted to see me, sir?"

"I know, I saw, Souta patched me through. Thank you for escorting him there. This is a priority, and I don't want to take any chances . . . It seemed to be a short interrogation, though," the chief observes.

"You informed me not to exhaust the witness, that he would be interrogated by the Ministry. I believe this has been their jurisdiction anyhow, sir."

"I know this is hard for you, Gwendolyn."

"Sir—"

"Gwen," the chief continues in a fatherly tone, "as you know, things are different in the Commerce Zone, more fluid. The Ministry wanted local Special Forces on this one. Less exposure, less public fear, resentment. There's a lot to take into account when you have the first entirely private police force. Especially on this island, people hate when Blue Jackets sniff around. They may have packaged the existence of all this as a necessity, some market inevitability, but it's still just an experiment; one that can go awfully wrong. I wanted you to interrogate him. I thought you might be able to extract information much easier and with much less severity than they could. They agreed to let you try."

"So you know . . . so they know we . . . ?"

"I don't presume either of you are simple enough to think I didn't know. It's my job to know what's going on in this department. And no, they only know that you brought him in, quickly and rather quietly."

"Is that why you put me on this case, sir?"

"You're on this case because you're the best officer I have right now, and I couldn't afford to fuck this up." The chief sighs. "They asked a lot of us. I trusted you not to disappoint."

Natal traces the wrinkles on the chief's somber face. "Don't worry about it, Gwendolyn, that's not why I brought you in here. Ministry Transpo has arrived. The director wants to meet you. And that's him right now, straight ahead. Look alive, commander." Natal shoots out of her chair and stands expectantly to the left of his desk.

"Thanks for the heads-up, sir," she jabs.

"You know I like to keep you on your toes."

"One last question, sir," Natal asks, as the director strides briskly and confidently toward them at the head of a group of formally dressed men in blue windbreakers with the word "Bureau" emblazoned in crimson on the right breast. "You always, me and Mi—Charles, sir, we're the only officers I've heard you call by first name."

"Why? I think that question answers itself."

The Director enters the room alone. Standing proud, his full stature occupies an ample amount of space. His legs appear shorter than his torso, which looks very well-fed. He seems fit, yet less fit than healthy.

"Hello, Mitch."

"Good to see you, Ben. This is Commander Natal."

The director steps directly in front of Natal, who leans back slightly and uncontrollably in response to his stature. He offers his giant hand, which engulfs Natal's. She is immediately caught off guard by his eyes, which look to have gone past exhaustion to a zombie-like state. Even more, they hold a wisdom and understanding that bores through Natal and immediately identifies her, indelibly classifies her, brands her. She feels uncomfortable and uncomfortably affixed to these eyes that she feels probing her, acquiring valuable and

55

personal information as if her own being was intimating details without permission.

"Thank you, commander, for your exemplary work." His voice is clear and precise. It carries. A semi-confident smile is all she can manage as she finally breaks from his gaze. "I have to ask. How did you know where to find the suspect?"

"Well, I didn't, sir. We had a minimal amount of leads which were being actively investigated. There's too much shrouded space to patrol effectively. We had tracking units, helicopters, the limited drone support allowed, but considering the suspect's background, I thought it best to try to catch the mouse when he left his hole.

"The timing was right for our fugitives to seek resources. We had two units frequenting localities, trying to flush them out, two units at the Ala Moana Mall. We stayed at Wahiawa. Contact, it's as vital, if not more so, than resources. Stealing a device means stealing a tracking device once reported. He wouldn't want to limit the range of his mobility. And, have you ever tried to ask someone to use their phone on this island? He didn't know where his face was posted; he would've wanted to get in and out. It's common knowledge there are no longer public phones on the island.

"Not much public anything," the chief adds.

"The outdoor malls are the only two places on this island that offer open public E-access. Ever since LE changed its name and set up corporate here, they shut down all locations except for the outdoor malls."

"Tourist booby traps," the chief offers with a smile.

"With the amount of people that frequent daily, and it being winter, it was the best place for us to hole up while I directed the search. It was a shot in the dark, sir."

"Well, you obviously have excellent eyes, aim is impeccable. I'm impressed, as I knew I'd be," the director compliments. "We'll be in contact," he says as he holds his hand out once more. This time he receives hers gently, his eyes still erudite and unreadable, but warm. Natal feels comforted and confused by the contrast.

"Alright, Mitch, I should be going," the director says, offering his hand now to the Chief. "Is the package ready?"

"Yes, sir. Paperwork's done. We have him waiting in a secure interrogation room as requested."

"Thanks, Mitch. Dependable as always," the director responds, while Natal observes the closeness of their relationship, a relationship previously unknown to her. "Sent some men down already, they should be in the process. I'm headed back to the convoy. Man, I hate being woken up."

"Like you sleep," the chief challenges, cracking the director's face, making both ends of his upper lip curl slightly into something close to a smile.

"See you soon, Mitch?"

"Count on it."

About five feet, from two confident steps, is how far the Director gets before the lights go off. Peering through the glass doors into the department, the chief watches as the lights are extinguished in sequential sections of rows, submerging the entire floor in darkness.

"Souta, what the hell is going on?" the chief shouts into his radio, before noticing he has no signal.

"Sir, we have to get you out of here," a medium-sized, stoutly built, square-jawed Blue Jacket asserts, appearing in the room almost instantaneously and looking resolute while he receives information by radio.

"Mitch."

"Ben," the chief barely responds before the director is through the double-glass doors that are held open to accommodate his robust frame, and whisked away by his entourage, leaving behind one Blue Jacket.

"I'm your communication channel, we're following through with retrieval," the Blue Jacket informs.

"Dammit—what the fuck's going on?" The chief laments after trying the backup frequency.

"Orders, sir?" Natal asks.

Her question immediately draws his attention as he focuses his eyes on her, making out her silhouette. "Charles is our immediate concern! Make contact with the transfer unit. Make sure the transfer is successful. I'll take care of everything else."

"Yes, sir," Natal dutifully responds, already heading for the door, leaving the Chief behind to coordinate.

"Can you get Bureau personnel to key locations? I need communication . . ."

Six

Charles is still meditating when he suddenly feels the brightness that engulfs him dissipate. Even with his eyes still closed he can feel the comfort of darkness shroud him. A shrill beep and a resounding click both emanating from the door serve as his cue. He gets up from his seat and slowly walks to the corner of the tiny room to the right of the door. There he kneels, trying to focus on details of the table and chairs, acclimating his eyes to the darkness.

Three Bureau agents make their way through the dark hallway. "We're still hearing shouts, the interrogation rooms are just ahead of us. That was gunfire . . . gunfire from above, I believe. Do you Copy? . . . The officer securing this location is with us now . . . alright, proceeding with retrieval," the trailing Blue Jacket says into his radio before again readying his firearm. "Best guess? Blackout. Convoy's fired up, orders are to expedite retrieval. Your chief's giving department-wide orders. You're to escort us out of the building and then resume post here."

"Orders received," the lone regular officer affirms while leading the group and feeling ill-equipped, despite his baton being set to high.

They reach the interrogation room, the third of four along the right side of the hall that leads to a dead end. Their escort, the officer, stands to the right of the door; the next in line takes position in front of the door, gun poised, while an agent behind him gives backup. Their commanding agent provides cover from the first of the interrogation rooms as he overviews the operation.

"Light's green on the door, sir," the agent facing the door relays.

"Are there different power sources feeding this place? Officer? . . . Officer?" the commanding agent asks.

"Uh, I think there's a backup generator that can keep vital access points, powered for a couple hours, sir," their escort finally responds.

"A couple hours—you think—you believe, huh? Does green mean open?"

"Yes."

"Why's the door open, officer?"

"I don't know. If there's power it shouldn't be."

"Whatever happened to keys and locks?"

"Just a routine pickup, huh, Boss?"

"Still a routine pickup, Waller. No time to be a smartass. If he wasn't here, we would've seen him leave. Proceed."

The officer places one hand on the door with gun still raised in the other and flings the door open. He storms the room only to have his wrist grabbed the moment it breaches. He is pulled forward, and turns just in time to witness a broad skull smash into his face. His eyes close and he lets off a shot. He feels one more forceful impact connect with his chin before he loses consciousness.

Charles quickly strips the agent of his firearm and manages to hoist him onto his shoulder. With gun pointed, he turns to his left and runs through the door and into the Blue Jacket waiting there. A shot rings out, and the Blue Jacket begins to crumple to the floor after a wretched wail from the bullet lodged in his thigh. Charles unloads the dead weight he carries onto him. The trailing Blue Jacket strenuously searches for a shot as all three men fall to the ground.

Charles tucks himself as close to the pair as possible, and takes aim at the regular officer who stands frozen with baton in hand. "Don't move," Charles whispers to the fallen agent who tries to roll the body off himself. "Drop your weapon or I'll shoot them," Charles shouts at the agent down the narrow hall.

"Shoot!" the agent replies, opening the steel door beside him for cover. "I'm not in the business of negotiating with terrorists!"

"Push that gun in your right hand aside," Charles dictates to the Blue Jacket beside him. "Do it!" He yells after several seconds of noncompliance. The agent yields, pushing it as far down the hall as he can. "Drop that," he dictates to their escort, who still stands, frozen. Slowly, the escort bends his knees and begins to place the baton on the ground, before flicking it with his wrist in Charles' direction.

The baton hits the ground, letting off a spark of electricity that briefly illuminates and intensifies the conflict, before rolling into the unconscious agent, who transmits and shares the shock he receives with his conterminous counterpart. Charles, still rolling away from the trouble spot, gets up to see the officer running toward the opposite end of the hall. Charles lets off a single shot, hitting the officer in his calf and collapsing him. "What you thinking about! Huh!" Charles screams, after grabbing and shutting off the baton by the neutral hilt. He hugs the opposing wall, making his way to the open door of his interrogation room for cover.

Ahead, he can hear the Blue Jacket attempting to communicate. He peers around the door, and with arms still bound lets off three shots into the steel door the commanding agent is behind.

"If you don't stop crawling!" He screams at the escort, who discreetly tries to slither his way along the floor toward the discarded weapon.

Behind cover, Charles scans the ceiling. He peeks around the door and begins to shoot at the piping above the Bureau agent. He dips back behind cover before the agent, who becomes aware of Charles' target, puts two bullets past him, embedding them in the concrete. Water begins to sputter down from the roof, prompting the agent to retreat into the room, closing the door soundly behind him.

Charles peeks out once more and gauges distance, then stands and heaves the baton with his shackled hands. He dashes to the escort, who has since ceased slithering. Charles grabs the key card attached to his side while the baton crackles and pops ahead, leaving a smoky mist that rises above the water.

Charles waits for the mist to abate then runs to the door that pens in the commanding agent, swiping the card and locking it. The handle jiggles violently, the pounds on the door are forceful, and then there's silence. He runs back to the guard, scavenging him for keys. He removes the cuffs with slight difficulty, while simultaneously hearing a key card gain access to the hall. He grabs the discarded weapon, runs to the door while it begins to open and, standing to its side, raises his gun to Commander Natal's head. Grabbing the gun from her hand, he nudges her inside and looks beyond the door. "You're alone?"

She gives no answer. "Third door," he says roughly. She takes in the chaotic scene as she walks and makes eye contact with the officer who now lies belly down. "Open it," he says once they reach the destination, pushing her inside once she completes the task.

Standing behind her, he leans forward slowly and kisses her softly on the back of the head. Swiveling, she turns and smacks him, leaving his face cocked at an angle. Her face fierce and flush with anger, he backs away, closing the door in front of him.

Inside the room, she hears a shrill beep and a resounding click both emanating from the door. She walks to the corner to the right of the door and sits, trying to make out details of the desk and chairs in the darkness. Her eyes ache from dryness.

Slinking around in the darkness, Charles takes care to avoid detection. The rowdiness above has spilled downstairs as Charles hears shouts, heavy steps, and general chaos all around. Working in the shadows, he clings to corners and cover, methodically making his way through the large Central Police Department.

He makes it to a side stairwell. Opening the door, he hears accented shouts and graphic protests in a different language coming from above. Lightly creeping up the staircase, he turns the corner to see an officer beating a man on the ground whom he towers over.

Charles sneaks up behind. While the officer cocks his arm back to deliver another blow, Charles wrests the baton from his relaxed grip and pressing it to his exposed neck, shocks him into incapacitation.

Looking down at the man who peers up at him through two bent, shaking arms, Charles shuts off the baton and drops it. He registers the man's large beard and blue jumper while he strips the officer and closely watches the man, who looks too frail and abused to move, try in vain to control his shaking while watching Charles circumspectly through his self-made cover.

Once changed, Charles slaps the helmet on his head and extends his arm, helping the man to his feet. He closes the visor and opens the door to the department floor. Dragging the officer out to a mass of cubicles, he tucks him beneath one and hustles through the grid of small offices to the door of the chief.

Opening the door slowly, he sees the chief staring straight at him while screaming into his radio. Charles lifts his visor. The chief is unable to maneuver away as the baton smacks into his right side, forcing a short curse from him before he drops to one knee in front of his desk.

The chief sits back and rests against his desk after the jolt. He watches as Charles slowly approaches.

"Howzit?" the chief asks in his usual baritone, his native accent briefly reigning over his voice.

"I've been better," Charles replies with gun aimed, stopping a few feet from his former chief.

"I didn't want to believe. This was all you, wasn't it?" The chief asks, calmly pressed against his desk.

"Friends in high places," Charles responds.

"What's the endgame?"

"We figure it out as we go. C'est la vie, no?"

"You don't know what you're doing. You're sick. You need help, Mike."

"I know what you're doing."

"What are you talking about?"

"I'm talking about what's going on above us; I'm talking about the Fifth Floor. I'm talking about the so-called Island Fever that's making zombies out of people."

Quiet pervades.

"These are government contracts, Mike, legit contracts. Yes, we temporarily house terrorists. This is just a way station."

"Bullshit! Official records might back you up, but I've read the memos, seen the video. Torture, experimentation, rampant abuse of every fucking code of ethics existent. What's going on?"

"Mike, you know you're like a son—"

"Stop with the bullshit, Mitch! What's going on here?"

"I don't know what you're talking about! You're sick, Mike! Aagghhh!" Mitch screams out as a bullet rips through his shoulder. "You fucking shot me!"

"I don't have time." Mike replies.

"It's a disease, Mike. People are getting sick; you're obviously sick."

"What did I just say?"

"Mike, listen; it's a combination of fluoride, mercury, some other things, I don't know exactly. It's the shit they're pumping in the air."

"What are you talking about?"

"The shit they're pumping in the air, LE, mixing with some stuff already here, floating around, and some stuff tailwind from out west, or the East, geographically—whatever. Over-industrialization in the area, a lot of science talk, blah-blah. There's just too much shit in the air," the chief concludes matter-of-factly.

"Bullshit, Mitch, I need proof."

"It's the truth, Mike. LE has all their top minds on it. They've already done a lot. The rate of mental lapses has decreased significantly. They're fixing it."

"By experimenting on people?"

"I honestly don't know what you're talking about—"

"How can you be so obtuse? No transparency, Mitch, none. That doesn't rub you wrong?"

"We were both soldiers, Mike. You've seen the world the way I have. Far from perfect, it's not held together by goodwill, universality, not lofty ideals; it's held together by string and a few pieces of used chewing gum. LE is that string right now. If this Commerce Zone fails . . . I don't know if I want to live in that world. We're the gum, Mike—at least you used to be."

"I need proof, records."

"I've told you this, Mike, because I want you to get better. Beyond that, I can't help you. If you can't trust my word then I think we're already done here."

"They're not your words," Mike says, then searches Mitch, relieving him of weapons and communication. He springs up, grabs the laptop from Mitch's desk and smashes the screen against the desk until it breaks off. Then, picking up a decorative letter opener from the desk, he pries open the base of the machine and extracts the hard drive, slipping it securely into his uniform pocket.

"So that was your play? They all took off once those cell doors opened." Charles doesn't engage. He looks through the blinds, checking the scene outside. "They've closed the perimeter, there's no way out, Mike." The side of the building is abuzz with authoritative bodies in motion. Walking back to the office door, he turns back to see his former chief, his former friend, sitting in the same place, calmly pensive.

"Don't do this, Mike," he pleads, the futility of the comment dripping from his voice.

"Thanks for everything, chief," Mike says. He presses the baton to the Chief's body, rendering him unconscious.

With darkness still shrouding him, he snakes through the cubicles to the facade-facing wall where he ducks under a windowsill. Discreetly looking up and over, he watches a joint operation as Blue Jackets direct personnel about the building's exterior.

Surreptitiously cracking the window ajar, he picks out a clear patch of grass and lets off several shots. Ducking down again, he rushes through the floor to the main staircase, walking past personnel on guard and out the door of the main lobby.

Outside he passes two standing guards, whose attention, like all others, is directed toward the suspect window. "Orders are being given," one declares, pointing him to a mass of uniforms on the perimeter of the lawn. Charles jogs briskly in

67

the direction.

". . . I'll say it again, containment is the objective. Nothing leaves this building." Charles waits as the agent assigns responsibility by groups. "You three, I need you on the right side of the building. Position yourself in the rear and give support," a Blue Jacket directs, pointing at Charles and two officers.

Charles immediately turns and begins running with the pack, making sure to position himself at the rear. Rounding the corner of the building, Charles slips away from the rest of the group, who continue to careen toward their destination. In his black uniform with tinted visor, he gives himself to the unpredictability and freedom of the night. . . .

Seven

. . . "So, you planned this all along?" the engineer asks as they descend from their campground. The slow drizzle dampens them.

"Not this, exactly."

"You did all that for a hard drive? What if there's nothing on it?"

"There's something on it. I was transitioning into computer systems. Chief trusted me. I've tinkered on it enough. He's on an entirely different network and there was enough security on his machine to protect a small bank vault."

The casuarina needles litter the earth, creating a light ecru-snowfield. Ironwood towers over them as they veer to the left, off the beaten path, and descend carefully down a steep decline to a trail of boulders along what looks like a dried-up stream.

"What are you trying to find?" The engineer manages to ask while concentrating on hopping to the next boulder.

"The original plan was networks, info, names, ISPS, anything usable, something that could help bypass proxies, ghosts, that was ideal," Mike explicates as he clears the boulder and grabs the engineer's arm to steady him for the drop. "Simply put, I know there are networks around that are hidden, protected. Have to crack them."

"How do you know they exist?" the engineer asks, less skeptical than quizzical.

"Stumbled onto one, accidentally. We cracked it. Didn't take long before we found video, email, all sorts of correspondence and info. Didn't take long before they found us. We got out in time, before they could pinpoint us."

"I'm sorry, but we? Us? Who?" the engineer inquires, as they traverse the last stretch of their descent, a field with few trees. Dead leaves, limbs, and twigs are strewn about and crunch under every step. The break of day offers faint illumination, barely giving the dark decay life enough to register.

Charles stops. He turns to meet the engineer's eyes. The engineer anxiously lowers his own eyes, then forcefully looks back, trying to maintain composure.

"I told you this morning that I got what I wanted, but it definitely wasn't the plan. You are not the plan. That morning, the train station, not the plan. I've seen what they do to people like you in "quarantine." It got the better of me. I just recently stopped questioning whether it should have.

"I am a criminal by law. I've been working with Anon. They were embedded, unnoticed, in the station's network. I caught on to them. They're untraceable. They caught on to me, and at first started to mock my efforts, navigating the systems seamlessly, with impunity. Then they began to show me things that took me a long time to believe. To them, maybe another part of the jest, to me it was education.

70

"I didn't divulge at first because I wanted to catch them. The challenge, I guess it fed my ego. I didn't divulge later because I didn't want them to be caught. We started correspondence, slowly at first. We built trust on both sides for almost a year. Then I told them about the mystery network. After that, it was the chief's hard drive. It was a simple plan, and then you happened.

"Now this is the part where I'm going to need an honest answer. I haven't told you anything that isn't known at this point, so there's nothing to find out. They'll see that. You don't have to stay. You can go back and tell them I held you after you came to your senses, and you got away when I was gone. I can make that look real," Charles says. The sheer intensity in his voice makes the engineer avert his eyes again. "But I do feel responsible for your situation. We're thirty feet away from the road, and the rest of this, and I'm not going to ask you to do anything unwillingly. So, what's your answer?"

The engineer looks down to the decay beneath him as it imperceptibly fertilizes the earth. "Honestly," he begins confidently, "I really don't have anything else to do. I mean, I don't really know myself, or feel like a self, I guess, is a better way to put it. Fuck. What's wrong with me?" An anxious sigh accompanies the jumbled attempt at elucidation. "This makes me feel at least like I'm doing something real, you know? I can't remember the last time I felt real, or like myself. I'll take this," he says finally, then walks past Charles to the road.

"I love you." Charles hears the whisper and immediately turns around. A familiar scent reaches him and dissipates through his body. Caught for a spell, he manages to tear himself away and follows the engineer's path to the road

71

ahead.

"What I'm trying to say is Adam Smith is not a god and capitalism shouldn't be a religion. You have a guy who made some really astute observations concerning nature, but he wasn't referring to a system of market manipulation and profit mongering. Here's a guy who wrote about moral sentiment. Why doesn't that ever come up when I hear defense for this globalized corporatocracy?"

"I don't have to defend capitalism; it defends itself. It works. Do you want to tell people what to do, professor? Are you comfortable with limiting an individual's potential for growth?"

"That has absolutely nothing to do with what I'm talking about! This system is unsustainable, the signs are everywhere. You can't dismiss that by labeling me an enemy of freedom. I'm not a lefty-liberal, neo-socialist, anti-democratic bogeyman."

"That's exactly what you are."

"And that's all the time we have for today. Thank you, gentleman, for—"

"I can't believe you just—"

"I'm sorry, Professor Campman, that's all our time. Thank you, Professor Campman, Congressman Lahey, for joining us to discuss this breaking controversy over Hindler's recent fraud investigation."

"I just think there will always be bad apples, Phil, and it's our job to pick them out so our system can continue working."

"Thank you for the wisdom, congressman. And that's all for Shaughnessy today. See you next time."

Disconcerted, the agitation is still apparent from the professor's dubious expression. Music begins to play, the Newsday anthem, as he watches Shaughnessy and the congressman exchange words and smiles that he imagines to be feigned and unintelligible gesturing.

"What?" Campman asks a face that peers at him.

"We've cut, you're clear. They yelled it."

Campman removes his mike, gets up and proceeds to exit the studio and headquarters until he emerges onto the New York City streets. He immediately starts dialing.

"Yeah, I know. I saw, I saw," is the introduction he receives.

"Doug, they completely spun it."

"To anyone that's not intelligent, Will."

"No one is."

"Will, I know, I know."

"I don't mean it like that, I didn't mean that," Campman says with more exasperation.

"You don't have to explain to me," Doug responds. "I get it. At least you're in a place to be heard, to actually say things."

"I know, you're right, it's just, being there, watching it happen. It's a little trippy, you know?"

Doug laughs, "I can imagine. I really like how they have these hosts with Irish-sounding last names. I guess they're going for the authenticity. You're the debate for the day, the guy with the other opinion. Now they can keep saying they're 'fair and balanced.'"

"Yeah, I get it, just had to vent, you know. I pretty much turned into a zombie after it ended, just sat there staring."

"I saw," Doug replies, chuckling.

"They had to tell me that it was over. I beelined for the exit. I'm happy I didn't come with anything; I must've walked out of there like Frankenstein's monster; I was so out of it," Campman jokes, eliciting another short chuckle from Doug. "Anyway, I decided right now to plan a talk in three months. I'm going to need a climate guy."

"You want me to be your climate guy?"

"I want you to be my climate guy. Is that good time?"

"What're we looking at?"

"Something like five spots, thirty minutes apiece, different issues," Campman explains as he finally begins to walk down the street, tired of being an obstacle on the busyish sidewalk.

"I'll be your climate guy."

"Thanks, as always. How's everything with you?"

"You know, same old."

"Yeah, seems like it only gets older."

"What can you do, right? How's . . . Uh, got to go, daughter, soccer. She's staring at me like I'm a horrible person."

"Yeah, always good talking to you, guy."

"Likewise, I'll be in touch. See you."

"Yeah," Campman replies as the phone clicks. He turns to the city that never sleeps and watches as women pose in boy shorts in an ad that transitions to a multicolored fleet of luxury hybrids, all projected on one of the many digital billboards hoisted up in Times Square. He decides that he's tired. He makes his way to the subway.

Walking through the main floor of the Central Police

Station, Natal tries her best to avoid the graphic that gyrates and turns on every computer screen. Entering the chief's office, she sees the stern-faced man with his left arm in a sling, staring intently at nothing.

"'Anon was a woman,' humph." The one-liner is exhaled, while the chief continues to stare as if trying to decipher some code in the thirteen characters. Natal allows the stout man time to assuage his grief while he is mesmerized by the visual that consumes his mind. She peers at the square man with the square jaw, broad brow and distinct facial features that are contradicted by his presently, soft, searching eyes.

"Definitely a hack sir," Natal relays. "Bureau techs are still working with our guys. They're trying to restore some kind of functionality to the network. A trace is unlikely, data looks to be a lost cause, but the backup drives are secure."

"They killed our radio frequencies. Wireless systems, networks, blah-blah, who the hell knows how any of this shit works? I never liked it, all this connectivity, just a big security risk."

"By the scale of the job, it looks like a hacker collective, sir. We're not sure if it's Anon. It seems there are a lot of copycats claiming affiliation nowadays, but more than likely, it was them."

"What do you know about them?"

"Not much, sir, we don't work computer crimes, you know. I probably haven't heard much more than you. Sprang up about three years ago, no one knows if there's any connection to Anonymous, speculation is it's a splinter cell or former members. They claim no affiliation. In any case, they've done some high-level jobs, stuff that makes this look like a joke.

There have been a couple raids, a couple arrests, but nothing too compromising.

"I have heard from someone, one of those jokes slash doomsday conspiracies circulating the web. Apparently some people believe it's some advanced AI gone wrong, some ever-evolving ghost in the machine. And everyone has an opinion on its intentions. Sounds like a joke, but if it's true . . ."

"Humph," the chief exhales again. "Who told you that?"

"Charles, sir," Natal states.

The chief leans back in his chair, his line of sight never wavering. His proud countenance looks beaten.

"The Bureau has taken over the case, as it should . . . as it should have. They've also taken over the Station. The Commissioner of Police and the Bureau Director have set up shop on the third floor; they'll be in and out. I'll be sitting here a while, just sitting. Do you understand, commander?"

"House arrest, sir?"

"At least I don't have a bracelet on my ankle. The Ministry will be sniffing around for a while."

"I'm sorry, sir."

"No need for apologies. You've always done your job admirably, commander." The chief breaks his stare, making eye contact with Natal. "I called you up here to let you know you're being temporarily transferred. The Bureau doesn't want to spend the time launching a new case. The Director has been looking into you; he wants you to continue under his command. Take the night off, you'll be reporting to him first thing in the morning, zero nine-hundred. If I were you, I'd consider this an audition."

Natal looks back blankly. All she can manage is a languid,

"Yes, sir," before the chief turns back to face nothing, focusing again on the mental imprint. She turns. She takes her time opening the door, aware she can't go back and wary of moving forward.

"Gwen, I'm sorry, for it all. Good luck."

"No need for apologies, sir." She stands in the doorway a moment, and then exits. She walks through the station floor registering the myriad colors that the graphic produces on every screen. Natal looks up at the large central screen that looms over the station floor, "Anon was a woman," she reads as the words bounce around. She wishes she was that woman.

A solemnness envelopes Gabriel as he and his date stroll along the Boulevard.

"Did you like the movie?" Alohi asks.

The wind gusts by, delivering a refreshing breeze that quenches like water. Alohi brushes her hair away from her face as it flutters about wildly. Gabriel plods along, careful to slow his pace, and enjoys the breeze that whips about his face and body, creating a comforting cocoon of air.

"It was alright," he answers nonchalantly. "Ward's getting huge."

"I like it, it's like they add something every other month. Now there's always something to do."

"Yeah," he responds as he registers her staring intently at him, her eyes tracing every line of his face. His straight nose comes to a distinct point; his dark eyes are brooding, as they never cease scanning. He turns to her and his attention leaves her flush.

"You're unique," she utters, wondering if her tan cheeks are turning red and noticing his jaw line that juts out into a sharp chin.

"Am I?" he retorts as they begin to walk over the short bridge that takes them to the other side of the street. He slows toward the middle of the bridge to watch the flood of vehicles speeding by. The clamor from the engines and the exhaust fumes from the hybrids congest the air.

"Yeah, you are. I like it," Alohi responds as nonchalant as possible. "You know people joke about you. They say you caught the Spooks," she says, smiling at him.

Gabriel looks first to the rain-soaked ground then glances to the clear, starless, night sky. "It hasn't really rained this winter," he comments, then slowly begins to walk ahead. She looks to the sky too, then follows.

"A couple big storms, there's some rain coming soon," she replies, and then looks around at the desolate walkway. "It'd be nice to see people on the street. I never see anyone walking anymore, especially at night."

"They're all driving," he responds.

She leans into him and puts her arm around his torso and her head on his shoulder. He puts his hand around her shoulder loosely, and then tightens his grip. They stroll along the walk, quietly passing by Kigelia, with their large sausage-like fruit dangling from thin vines and their nighttime blooms beginning to show. They saunter by Indian coral, their radiant flowers giving life to the night sky. They walk along the sidewalk of the multiple-lane Boulevard until they are across from the Ala Moana mall, where Alohi stops.

"You sure you don't have to get home?" Gabriel asks.

"No, I told you both my parents work nights."

"What's up?" Gabriel asks while looking across the street at the illuminated complex.

"Let's go to the beach," Alohi says excitedly.

"Beach Park is closed. You know how much they patrol for the homeless."

"We're not homeless."

"It's still closed to us."

"Aye, boy, you chicken? I don' think you were," Alohi teases, allowing her attenuated accent to slip at leisure.

Gabriel looks at her face bubbling with enthusiasm, thoughts of revelry twinkling in her eyes.

"Let's go," she baits.

Eight

Walking together, toward the beach, Gabriel holds Alohi's wrist loosely but securely. Comforted by the gesture, she walks by his side through the banyan trees. He tugs firmly and they both dart behind a tree and kneel, avoiding the lights of an oncoming vehicle. Peeking through the mass of roots, Gabriel watches the car while feeling Alohi's body nestle into his own.

"It's a regular car," he informs, while standing. Slowly, she rises and intertwines her hand in his. He makes no attempt to protest. They continue to walk through the short field.

"We'll just tell them we really wanted to see the beach. That it won't happen again. They won't arrest us."

"We look local, they might, and they'll definitely give us trespassing violations. I don't want to deal with any of that," he explains resolutely.

At the end of the field, they look in both directions before crossing and dart through the opening of a tall wall that sections off this part of the coast. Down a short series of steps and to the left, Alohi leads them to the wall, where she sits and leans her back against it and tries to pull Gabriel down with her.

He allows her to and leans back to witness the rolling ocean crash down on itself. The dark sky is brightened by a clear moon, and the blue-blackness sedates him.

"Before they raised this wall you could see much more from the street. And you already had to sneak in here at night. It doesn't make sense," Alohi says to the wind, which blows heavily and carries the lament away.

"Not much on this Island that makes sense anymore."

"Makiki, it's one of the last places on the west side that still has community," she says.

"That's because a president grew up there. It can't be the same as it was before. I'm tired of the tourists with their cameras all over my street."

"I know, but still. Compared to the rest of the Island, ya' know. I want to move windward. At least some parts are still nice over there, residential, not too fake or done up."

"Why not another island? Another country?"

"I guess I love it here. I grew up here. Maybe it'll change, but I doubt it. And the other islands are all bought up. Corporate Farming's everywhere, don't think I want to live in that. This is bad enough."

"I never knew you thought about shit like that."

"You never knew me," she replies, and again nestles into his torso, this time without interruption. "But I know you, you're a genius. The quiet act doesn't fool me."

"What?"

Alohi laughs. "I'm interested, how did you get your name? You look more local than most. Is it the angel? That's a little cheesy . . ."

Gabriel smiles. "My mother loves to read. It's really all she

81

does besides work. She named me after a favorite author."

"Who?"

"Gabriel Garcia Marquez."

"I love him, *Love in the Time of Cholera*."

"*100 Years of Solitude*."

"They can be if you let them . . ." Alohi says. "Are your parents local?" she asks after a moment of silence, only to receive another.

"I never knew my father, but both my parents were . . . What about you? You look pretty mixed up. How'd you get your name?"

"Well, I am all mixed up—Tahitian, Filipino, Japanese, German, some Irish and French in there, probably some other stuff, and a lot of Hawaiian. I was actually named after my great-great-grandmother," she laughs briefly. "My mother always tells me that only the haoles say 'Aloha' anymore, and if she didn't think it was so silly, she would've named me Aloha just to hear locals say it. So she went with Alohi. I think it's silly that she still thinks there are locals."

"Does it mean anything?"

"Shining."

"You are pretty shiny, can't really look right at you." The flattery comes almost involuntarily. *Why did I say that?* he thinks.

"You think so?" she asks as she rights herself and rolls over to straddle Gabriel. "Am I glistening?" she asks Gabriel, who looks but is not present.

His mind conjures a memory of one dove chasing another in a circle, at the very same beach. He always imagined it was a male chasing a female, continually, incessantly. *The mating game*, he thinks. *How can he catch her?* Circumference, distance of circular motion is equal to linear motion, equations, math begins to consume his thought processes. *He has to keep her in the same circle, keep her interested, 2 * pi * r/T. And then, he has to cross D = C/pi.* The thoughts crash down and roar like the ocean.

Alohi unzips her hoodie, revealing a low cut tee. "Am I shimmering?" she asks Gabriel, and then dips her head to meet his lips with hers.

Gabriel participates physically and calculates mentally. *But if he moves too fast he'll crash into her, (u+v)/2,* he thinks as he bites down on her lip.

"I'm sorry. You alright?" Gabriel asks Alohi, who raises her hand to her lower lip.

"It's alright, it's alright, it was just a little hard. I'm fine," she says as she dips her head again.

"Nah, no. Stop. Stop, I got to go."

"What's wrong?"

"I just . . . I gotta go," Gabriel mumbles, while gently guiding her off of him. He stands hurriedly; sand falls from his backside. He scales steps by twos, and is gone. *But if he crashes, if he realizes that as just an obstacle, mindless pursuit, he can learn to fly, Cl * 1/2pV2 * S. He can soar, and eventually, learn to reach the stratosphere, space Δv = veln * mss0/mss1, the heavens.*

His headspace is flooded as he begins to run, *And maybe he can transcend time, dimension.* Gabriel stops and drops to his knees before a banyan tree. Both palms rest firmly on the ground as he tries to root himself. In vain, he tries to quiet the tempest of thought that storms in his head.

83

The third floor, Department Offices, was the last floor she was granted admission by her clearance. The fourth floor, Documents and Records, and the fifth floor, Storage, were well above her clearance, a verity only recently questioned.

Natal steps off the elevator onto the third floor. Two rights take her down a narrow hall with offices on both sides. The clear windows and doors assure mutual accountability, as she and those she walks by maintain composure. Another left at the end of the hall and a short walk bring her to an office occupying the end of a larger hall. It's the only office with a wood door and an opaque window, the commissioner's office.

To the best of her knowledge, this office is usually empty, a department formality, a satellite location rarely used, snubbed for an office at City Hall. She knocks courteously, but forcibly on the solid oak door.

"Come in."

She opens the door to see the commissioner sitting behind a heavy oak desk. She can tell he has just lifted his head from the mountain of paperwork before him. To her right, she sees the Bureau director.

"Excuse me, Commissioner Patao, but an appointment has arrived. Is it possible—"

"Of course, Director, I have some pressing matters to look into presently, anyhow," the commissioner responds, while standing and checking his phone. He passes by Natal, who makes room for his exit. His eyes are glossed over, and he offers no words of departure, but steals a lengthy glance of Natal as he passes.

"Please, close the door, commander."

Natal shuts the door, and stands poised before it. "Have a seat, commander. Relax."

She walks in, noticing the warmly decorated office, the burgundy carpet, oak furnishings inclusive of bookshelves, the jade lamps, and the contradiction presented by the black metal desk the director now directs from. He depresses an office chair that looks strained by the weight.

"Internal Audits and Inspections from local PD and the Bureau are here. Commissioner Patao and I have to oversee all investigations respectively, so we've given office hours. That explains why you and I are here now, commander," the director relates.

Commander Natal tries to avoid his eyes that continually attempt to bore though her. "The Bureau respects results and you've given them. The Bureau also expects results. I want you to take your team. I have two agents for you. I want Charles caught. You and your assisting Commander will meet them at Bureau headquarters in the Ministry. You'll be giving orders, commander," the director informs, then gives Natal a stare that magnetically attracts her line of sight. She looks into his eyes and focuses on not becoming consumed by them. "You'll have every resource needed. Call me personally with any requests," he says, placing his card on the desk. "I have your case briefing, do you have an operations briefing for me, commander?"

"Yes," Natal says, placing the two manila folders she holds on his desk, and taking his card in the process. "They're both there."

"Do you have any questions, commander?"

The calm intensity of his gaze implores Natal to tense, to err, to forfeit her character in any way to his judgment. "Do you like it here, sir?" she asks warmly.

His brow furrows and then relaxes, along with the rest of his face where just a hint of a smile is present. "Honestly? Not particularly," he admits, after getting up and proceeding to the opposite side of the room. "Would you like a drink, commander?" he asks, en route to the bar. He appears as if he's concentrating on not shaking the ground as he walks.

"Thank you, but no, sir."

"Well, the commissioner offered, so I intend to take him up on that offer. You were Military Special Operations, am I right, commander?"

"Yes, sir."

"Can I ask for your judgment, commander?"

"Of course, sir."

"Do you think he looked annoyed when he left?"

"I think he looked like he didn't want to be, sir."

The Director pours two glasses of whiskey. He walks them back to his desk and places one in front of Natal. "I like that answer, commander, but sometimes no is not an answer. I can't drink alone." The Director sits and raises his glass. Natal follows suit. He takes a healthy gulp, Natal a sip. "As commissioner, his position has become largely ceremonial. I think this is the most work he's done in years. It also doesn't help to be sharing an office. I don't like the quiet, but I like the work atmosphere it produces."

He leans back in his chair and takes another gulp.

"You were born on this island. Do you consider yourself local, commander?"

"My mother considered us local, sir."

"And you?"

"I believe in this community, sir," she responds.

"Your mother was of Japanese descent, and your father was born in Korea; am I correct?"

"Yes, sir."

"Your mother passed from cancer when you were in your teens?"

"Yes, sir." she replies, now looking at him with an almost imperceptible, incredulous expression.

"And your father was a victim of violent crime much earlier. Is that what drives you, Commander?"

"Among other things, sir," she answers, now meeting his eyes ardently. The director remains equable and visually dispassionate.

"I'm sorry for your loss, commander." The comment enigmatically borders both the genuine and phlegmatic. "Do you know how long I've been director?" he continues.

"Seven years, I believe, sir."

"Seven years. Seven relatively peaceful, calm years. This Commerce Zone has existed now for thirteen. I see you've been with us for five. Do you know what it was like ten years ago?"

"Not first hand, sir."

"It was hard, commander. When all this started, everyone thought the world was coming to an end. It wasn't a doomsday conspiracy this time, though. It was economic collapse and international tension.

"When LE got the contract to govern this place you can imagine it didn't go over well with the indigenous population.

They were only about seven percent, poor, violent, but the locals identified with them. Together, that accounted for roughly seventeen percent. LE thought they could keep the social structure, just manage it, they thought it would be an accepted transition. It wasn't. The people here still weren't over being part of the States. 'Our island is sold.' I'm sure you've heard the rallying cry, seen the posters. There were protests, mobs, riots. Crime became rampant. The police did nothing because they were them.

"So—solutions, Ministries, a more streamlined force. Military recruits, specialized training, not deadly, but overwhelming force. Which is why only commanders carry firearms. These are the changes I oversaw when I was brought in as Director of Security.

"We were able to quell the mini-revolution but not the resentment. There was so much resentment lingering it bubbled over, turned to terrorism. We've got every country and entity that depends on this zone looking out for the innumerable that want to blow this place sky high, but domestically . . . Homegrown terror, it wasn't too smart or organized. It was scary. There were a number of attacks and then the tourist bus bombings.

"That's when I started the Bureau, 2030. Within months, we hushed all the terror talk and now this is one of the safest places in the world.

"I tell you all this because I don't sit at this desk now, I haven't put in all this work for this Commerce Zone because I want to, or because I have to, but because I'm willing. I'm willing to do what needs to be done." The Director takes another large gulp, draining the glass. He leans forward in his chair again, his forearms resting comfortably on the chair arms, causing his shoulders to hunch. "And I surround myself with those same people. You seem like one of those people, commander. Are you?"

"Yes, sir," she replies sternly. Even now, less radiant, with her countenance dimming, she remains stunning, alluring.

"This is a significant breach. If this goes over my head it falls in the lap of a private firm, and it will get done. We have to prove that we can secure ourselves. I'll shore things up on this end. I'm relying on you to take care of the rest. Are you willing, commander?"

"Yes, sir."

"Good. Clearances will be given when you arrive at headquarters, along with a full case briefing. You're expected in two hours. Are you prepared, commander?"

"Yes, sir."

"Then you are dismissed, commander . . . and, commander, I feel I'm a very good judge of character. I'm sure you'll prove me right," the director says to a standing Natal. She nods gently, and then turns.

"What we have here isn't a system of economy, what has been globalized isn't commerce, it's our unequal system of access and exploitation . . . " Professor Campman looks through the audience while he speaks. He always likes to study the faces of those who sit and ingest his brand of reality. He knows they are all of a similar mind, but not the same mind, not the same comprehension, not the same willingness or ability to affect difference, let alone change.

There are the retirees, he thinks, not too keen on using old or elderly. The 'lifers,' he dubs them, because, he believes, few change their ideology in old age, and he knew even those few didn't come to these talks. These are the lifetime advocates, probably activists, who came with his book in their possession. They are more studious than attentive. To Campman, they had all long since moved past lifestyle differences and now bear a collective sense of unfulfilled responsibility, appearing as if they have relieved Atlas of his duty. They are sprinkled through the audience, a small percentage, rarely with company. *This is what I did. What more can I do?* He imagines them thinking.

" . . . The math doesn't add up. The bubble burst years ago, yet we continue to travel through the same ideological minefield. Poverty and homelessness are at statistical highs. The unemployment rate is inflated with the proliferation of labor jobs, while the average worker cannot support themselves.

"This downward spiral isn't another economic roller coaster. The bourgeois movement is dead. There is no longer a middle class because their system can't use them anymore. Now there are only the homeless, the workers, and the wealthy, a complete paradigm shift . . ."

Then there is what he likes to call the mid-list, because he thinks the people in the middle of their lives are so different, so varied, so ideologically fragmented. They are almost all professionals. He thinks he can identify with near certainty their profession. He figures they are mostly teachers, or better yet, academics. He goes down the list; *teacher, sorry, academic, academic, lawyer, hmm, artist, academic, laborer.* Every individual asks something different with their eyes, seeks the answer they want in his words.

Sorry officer, he catches himself thinking to a shaking head, *but I do think unions can be destructive, don't mean I think they should be destroyed.* There are those that see the cause above all else, but the midlist, he thinks, harbors the most with their own agenda, the most that come to judge and not be judged.

" . . . And it's still only the rich and the wretched poor that are subsidized in this welfare state. The poor are locked into the worst system of government dependence and debt leverage ever, while the rich enjoy a gilded age of investment and transaction deregulation.

"Everything has been privatized. A tax-free, tariff-free zone, on a privately managed and secured island that is still legally part of a state, isn't economics. Zone C. Commerce Zone. Free trade, they claim, for what is just another disgusting precedent, a victory for the opportunistic and exploitative globalist."

He looks now for his favorite group. Through the disparaging and shocked faces that actively label him radical, through the stern and contemplative faces that desire to look unaffected, he finds the nodding heads, the faces aglow, which are unable to resist expression. These faces belong mostly to the youth.

Emotion, this is what he enjoys the most about the youth, that uncompromising sense of self. That trust in the vibration of their own bones which allows them to be present and honest emotionally. Perusing, he sees the diversity of possibilities. Some are trying to figure out this life, some have just begun trying to live one, some, he can only imagine.

How did they all get here? He thinks. *How could they not?* He watched all but a few drift in and out when he spoke on mathematics, theory, history. Still, he can see that the issues resonate, and that this group trusts the vibration.

The youth—the future—they are what keep him going, who he directs his words at, making sure to leave the door open so the past and present can listen in. He relishes in the fact that the more honest he is with himself, the more radical others claim him to be, the more of the future he sees before him each time he speaks.

"This is not a system that can be sustained; it hasn't been for some time now. Instead, it's been managed."

These faces, individuals unabashed, unconstricted, unlimited, is how he thinks of them, as the infinite. *Him and him and her*, he thinks as he wades through the ocean of faces, until a face in the crowd brings cause to pause.

The man looks to be in his late thirties. He's pensive, yet relaxed. His eyes are bagged and relentless, and he fills the auditorium seat snuggly as he peers at Campman like a hunter unwilling to lose his prey.

Campman has seen this man before, sometimes bearded, sometimes nearly bald, but always with the same eyes which were never as intense as they seem today. It's the fourth time Campman recalls seeing the man who has never tried to meet him. Today the professor feels something in those eyes he can't place, something that's trying to be communicated.

"This is the reality in which we exist, and something must be done about it. Interconnectivity threatens to submerge us all in our current state. This system will continue to polarize classes until it collapses us all under the weight of its failure."

The man's eyes haven't wavered, and don't now as Campman turns to leave the podium, receiving a healthy round of applause as he goes.

"Still no time for a 'meet & greet?'" the production assistant asks.

"Still got to meet the family for dinner, my son just won a championship."

"Really? You must be proud. What sport?"

"Basketball. Is there any other?"

The assistant laughs, throwing back her slim, scholarly face. "You *are* proud. Thanks for giving the short talk, professor."

"Anytime. Sorry if it turned into a bit of a sermon."

"Not at all, they want someone to say it, even if they act like they don't. They're eating it up. You're becoming quite the nerd celebrity, professor," the assistant adds, still smiling.

Campman can't help but laugh. "Trust me, the groupies are not the same. Mine are so much better. They do stuff like read my kids to sleep so my wife and I don't have to."

The bit produces a good amount of laughter. "I'm sure. Have a good night, professor."

"You too," Campman replies. He walks to a nearby chair to retrieve his bag and coat.

"Congratulations!" she adds.

"Thank you," he replies. Slinging the strap of the bag over his right shoulder, he hurries to the door.

"Yeah, I'm a little early. Are the kids ready?" Campman says aloud as he drives on the highway.

"Yeah, they're flying around as usual, but they're ready to go."

"Alright, I'll be there in a bit."

"How was the talk?"

"Good, interesting crowd for a university talk, healthy crowd for a university talk."

"People like you, babe."

"Yeah, well, what do they know that you don't?"

"I don't like you 'cause I love you. With you, those can't coexist. See you soon?"

"See me soon, love you too, hun," Campman says, transmitting his usual charismatic smile through the line, and with the push of a button on the steering wheel, he kills it.

"Call ended," a pleasant female voice informs him as he tries not to become mesmerized by the road. He checks his rearview, ready to give up his comfortable pace today for the convenience of speed. Before turning, he spots a black Lincoln town car driving two cars behind him, in the lane to his right.

In the fast lane, he whizzes by the median, now anxious to see his family. His Chevy Pulse quickly catches up to the car ahead of him, and his right blinker telegraphs his intention. Merging in the right lane, he takes one more glance in the rearview. He can't help but notice the Lincoln emerge from the fast lane, two cars behind him, and merge in to his current lane. He watches it driving a car behind him before he re-enters the fast lane.

Now flying down the highway, he looks at his right side mirror. He sees the Lincoln merge from two lanes over into the lane to his right. Now beside him, and a healthy car length behind, he can't help but feel the Lincoln is trying to match his speed.

He drives two lanes over, slowing down in the process. Unsurprisingly, he catches the Lincoln drop behind him, until it merges in the lane beside him, remaining one car behind.

Campman, emboldened by the discovery and unsure of the best plan of action, slows. Now beside the Lincoln, he looks to the tinted black passenger window, needing to discover what's behind the darkness.

He rolls down his window and screams at the tint. "Why are you following me!" No response. He honks his horn and howls, "Why are you following me!"

Slowly, the Lincoln's passenger window rolls down, and those same eyes track him. "Why are you following me?" Again, he receives no response, just two unrelenting eyes that slowly disappear behind the tinted window. Campman accelerates, taking the next exit too fast, forcing him to break and turn wildly to avoid slamming into the guard rail. Once off the highway, he pulls over immediately.

With both hands affixed to the wheel, his heart, engorged with blood, thumps inside his chest. He breathes deeply while his mind races. *What the hell was that—some kind of message? Who the hell was that?* He sits stuck, staring at and into nothing. *The eyes of a hunter. He was marking me,* Campman thinks. *He wants me to know I've been marked, that I'm prey.*

Campman takes a deep breath and leans back in his seat. Five minutes later, he would drive home, making sure not to see any Lincolns in the process.

Nine

"Because I love you, that's it, no other reason."

"That's not fair. This doesn't mean I don't love you. F-R-Q-P-S-L . . ."

This is where they would often end, phantom memories, ending with a name caught by the wind before he could speak it. He would go through the alphabet trying to conjure it, to no avail. Every broken dream became a testament to a broken mind. Every fragmented delusion, every ethereal image that felt almost tangible, shattered, and left in its wake a reality that he couldn't trust, let alone believe—the phantoms haunted.

"What is this?" Charles mumbles.

"What is what?" the engineer asks.

"Nothing," Charles responds, waking from his dream world and reclaiming his mind. "If we just keep walking, we should get there soon."

"Right, should be where? Should be where soon? Some geographical dot on the globe that you deciphered from some cryptic email?"

"Don't! Not now."

"Sorry, sorry, you know how I get. Sorry. We've just been

walking for half a day through the wild to a thing I never knew existed. We left our transportation—"

"Honestly, how many things you think exist that you don't know about? The worst thing that could happen right now is some flying robot finding us. Those mopeds are no use to us anymore without a plan. You're free to walk anywhere you want. I just don't want to hear about it."

"You're right, I know, I'm sorry. It's just that I've been following . . . it's frustrating not having control of anything. Then there's a part of me that's just so irritable, it's like I'm two different people. I get so confused sometimes, and then it comes out."

"What feels realer, what feels more like you?"

"Honestly? . . . It does. If there is something else, it feels like a shell was built around it, and I'm that shell. But there's something natural about it. It doesn't feel good, not horrible exactly, but not good. I don't like the feeling, when it . . . I don't . . . I can't even explain it. But, it's honest, like that's real and I'm not."

"Kind of confusing," Charles offers.

"Kinda fucked."

"You never really answered me. Do you have thoughts, dreams . . . they seem like they're real . . ."

"Like—like they're real and I'm fake?"

"Sounds tough."

"I'm sure you'd know."

An hour of silent trekking later, they emerge from the woods onto a road. The newly setting sun still produces an orange glow, abating the purple dim of dusk. The heavy clouds overhead threaten to rain.

97

The seemingly endless, narrow road, is a one-street shantytown. Beat and rusted automobiles are scattered along both dirty sand-walks. Makeshift tents of all sizes and materials are strewn about, some tucked among the thin woods. The shanty residents walk about in various states of disrepair, tending to their daily activities. They perch, sit, walk, barter. Charles watches one retrieving laundry from a tree branch.

"I've heard about this place. Is this for real?" the engineer asks.

"Never seen it? It's only grown over the years. The first time I saw this place was years ago, when I was just visiting. It was crazy then, but nothing like this. I always wonder why LE doesn't clean this place up. I guess there's a certain logic to allowing this to exist," Charles finishes in a whisper.

"You sure we're in the right place?" the engineer asks, while Charles pulls a map from his pocket.

"Just follow me." Two hundred yards down the phantasmagoric stretch, they witness a society unchained. Liberal mentalities interact deliberately and silently, and stare cautiously at them until they take a left. A hundred thirty odd more yards, and they come upon another cluster of tents within the thin woods.

Charles looks about and points at a multicolored tent, one side forest green, and the other black. "There," he says to the engineer. Slowly, they approach. The engineer looks at the group of tents, wondering why this specific area of the shanty seems devoid of life. They round the tent and reach the front. On the proverbial doorstep of the mobile home, they glance at each other.

"Hello," Charles greets, turning toward the tent. Night is burgeoning; last light and the approach of the darkening world lend an eerie calm to the quiet community.

"Hello," greets an emotionless voice from within.

"I'm a friend," Charles continues.

"Welcome, friend," the voice calls out, now inviting.

The large tent flap begins to open. As it seemingly unzips endlessly, the two fugitives begin to register artificial and fluorescent light. With the opening clear, they face a slender, short man with glasses. His plaid shirt is wrinkled about the collar and unbuttoned, revealing a sweaty crew-neck tee. His jeans are slightly baggy and tucked into worn but expensive hiking boots. His face looks young, but his eyes are stern.

Charles looks beyond him and sees a caged fluorescent bulb hanging from the roof of the tent, irradiating the entire enclave. A single wire hangs down from the light and trails along the matted ground until it finds its home in an enormous generator, from which sprout numerous other wires like roots, some of which Charles follows until they disappear into the ground through cut sections of matting. One in particular runs to the right side of the tent where it becomes an outlet box. Two extension cords are plugged into this outlet, and numerous cords into those extensions, transferring the energy that powers the mass of screens and towers running silently.

"What the fuck?" Charles hears the engineer behind him.

"Come in, friends are always welcome. You can call me Jay."

"I'm—"

"Mike. I know about you and your friend. I've been expecting you. I'm what we call a cell moderator, one of them, at least. I pretty much oversee operations here."

"What is this place?" the engineer asks, now inside and looking about quizzically.

"Well, it's a community of truly like-minded people. It's complicated, something that probably isn't too easily explained. In short, this is a social contract for a certain way of living. Even shorter, this is a mobile hack station, a cell of Anon," Jay answers, closing the tent.

"Habit of talking in riddles? Definitely a hacker. I take it all the tents around here are similarly decked out, and they're all connected to this central generator?"

"Very deductive, Commander Charles. Sorry, Mr. Charles."

"Call me what you want. It must be tricky keeping this hotspot cool. Can I ask how many tents you have in this community?" Above, rain faintly showers the tent top.

"No need to go too far, too soon, Mike. I'm sure you'll find out what you want to know in time. You're here to make contact, though; am I right? Just walk this way."

Before Jay has time to reach his keyboard, he registers a message on his screen. Skimming the lines, he turns to Charles. "Can't be. I think this is also for you." Mike walks to the screen and reads the message.

Prometheus Unbound
Man look to the night sky while light still affords industry
Drone watch by moonlight
Follow Mr. Grey

"This isn't real," Jay says, shocked.
Mike rushes to the tent opening. Outside, he stares at the

sky, turning and peering. Darkness threatens to consume the night sky; only a dull purple glow is present on the horizon. Mike rushes back inside the tent. "Get your people out, you're compromised."

"Prometheus is Unbound. The message is out." Jay responds, as a man wearing a grey coat walks into the tent.

"Hey, time to go," he says staring at the bunch.

"Who the fuck is this?" the engineer asks.

"Get out of here!" Jay screams.

"It's time to get out of here," the new arrival yells again.

"What the hell?" the engineer yells.

"We gotta go! Let's go! Let's go!" Mike shouts, ushering the engineer out by the shoulders. At the entrance he turns back to Jay, who furiously click-clacks away on his silent keyboard.

"You coming? We gotta go now!" Mike shouts to his back.

"Can't do that, we have protocol," he explains without turning.

Mike storms out the tent, catching up to his troop. The sky has opened up and he is immediately dripping.

"Where's Jay?" the engineer asks.

"Don't worry about it, just keep moving!" Mike bellows ahead.

"Just follow me!" Mr. Grey yells. Soon they're accompanied by a torrent of people sprinting from the direction they fled. "Don't get lost in the crowd. Follow me!"

Mike hears a heavy boom. Nearly roadside, he turns to witness the aftermath of a small explosion. They all watch as the tent city is set ablaze, tent by charring tent defying the weather and becoming food for flame as Prometheus makes his entrance.

101

"Keep moving!" Mike shouts.

"This way!" Mr. Grey commands, as he turns and sprints down the road. In the distance sirens can be heard. All about them, dilapidated vehicles come alive, betraying their true condition. Engines roar and tires screech as vehicles peel out in droves.

"Here!" Mr. Grey yells, as they reach a large, dark-turquoise truck equipped with off-road tires. "Get in!" Before Charles can acquiesce, he sees a light launched from the campsite shoot through the air and then burst like a firecracker, illuminating all. In the distance, against the momentarily illuminated backdrop, he barely makes out an object fall from the sky. "Get in!" Mr. Grey insists.

Charles hops into the passenger seat, and the vehicle roars to life. He slams the door shut. The rain abates but continues to shower down. "Some sort of EMP?" he asks, as he hears the engineer slam the rear door.

"Yeah, there'll be more surveillance on the way." Mr. Grey answers.

"I'd like to see the weapon that fired that." Charles confesses.

En masse, the flock of vehicles flies down the road. The confluence merges seamlessly, flooding the road and flowing rapidly. They are near the head of the pack and flanked on all sides by the new refugees.

"Not exactly how things were supposed to go, but at least we're not alone," Mr. Grey comments.

The sirens get louder. "Road block ahead," Charles informs, as he spots a row of blue and red lights across the road ahead. "Looks like they're trying to double up," he conjectures, before they hear a large crack followed by a crunch.

"They're overrunning it," Mr. Grey states. They hear another loud crack. The sound of vehicles colliding becomes prevalent. Shots begin to ring out.

"What's happening!" the engineer screams from the backseat.

"Get down!" Charles shouts.

They reach the bottleneck of the blockade, where the vehicles ahead created a single narrow lane for them to navigate. Charles sees two rows of police and Bureau vehicles on both sides of the road; some smashed into tents or rundown vehicles, some smashed into by runaways. Armed authority lines the road and fires shots at passing cars, running into the thin woods whenever renegade vehicles veer toward them. A shot rips through the truck body, the back window shatters.

"Fuck! Fuck! Fuck!" the engineer screams.

"Are you hit!" Charles asks, hunched, but with eye line above the dash, unwilling or unable to forfeit the advantage of sight.

"No! No!" the engineer answers.

"I'm not asking again!" Charles screams back. Once through the thick, they emerge with a thinner flock of vehicles. Behind, shots continue to ring out, some in their direction. Ahead, more police units threaten to converge.

"We're taking a left!" Mr. Grey yells.

"Just along for the ride!" Charles replies.

Ahead, at the first turn, the group begins to split in the only available directions, left or straight.

Cars weave as police spontaneously try to create

blockades. One cruiser heads straight for them.

"What the fuck is he doing!" Mr. Grey screams.

"Just go straight!" Charles yells.

"What?"

"Just go straight!"

"Shit," Mr. Grey exclaims as he continues ahead. The windshield wipers slam against the windshield as they swing rapidly.

At the last moment, the police unit swerves, leaving its backside directly in their path. They ram into it at high speed, spinning it. The truck swerves, threatening to flip. Mr. Grey works the wheel, attempting to right them. The right side of the vehicle slams into another refugee, assisting with balance and Mr. Grey slows, then accelerates into a sharp left, rejoining a small group of cars.

"Shit!" Mr. Grey screams.

"Fuck!" the engineer screams, finally coming up for air.

"You're a pretty good driver!" Charles compliments.

Two hundred yards down the road, among a mass of vehicles and with the police again ahead of them, Mr. Grey takes a sharp left straight into the woods, barely catching a path that's as much trail as road. In the darkness, he expertly navigates through the wooded area.

"Familiar with these parts?" Charles asks.

"You can say that," Mr. Grey answers. "Relax and enjoy the ride, fellas. We'll be on foot soon."

"Yes, looks like a hacker cell, sir . . . Yes, sir, nine perp casualties, maybe a couple self-inflicted, eleven prisoners, six injured, sir. No ministry casualties, five injured."

"Don't worry about it, agent. There'll be a cleanup crew there shortly. Good intuition, we're still trying to find out how these people operate. Anything recovered?" the Bureau director inquires.

"No, sir, they appear to be very organized. Destroyed everything," Natal replies, squinting, then turns her back to the morning sun. "That escape appears to have been a decoy. We've found tracks that disappear into the woods. Probably core members."

"And information. We've been getting lazy, stagnant. For this to be happening under our nose . . . It's an embarrassment to the Bureau. You're a breath of fresh air sorely needed, agent."

"Excuse me, sir?"

"Yes?"

"You keep calling me 'agent,' sir."

"It's not a mistake, Agent Natal. After today, you deserve it. Good job directing the raid. I want you to continue pursuing our fugitives; I need you to wrap this up, agent. Leave the incident site to me, understood?"

"Yes, sir," Natal replies before hearing the click of the phone. She walks back toward the three agents who wait behind the last car in their four-vehicle entourage.

"At least no one got head-butted this time," Jezequel greets with a smirk.

"We're moving out, I'm giving orders by radio," Natal commands, walking past them to her own vehicle.

"Comply! Comply!" she hears. An agent points his gun at a shanty resident and tries to verbally halt his advance. The man, who jumped out of the pen that was created for the residents, walks toward the agent with no indication of intention. "Stop or I will shoot!" the agent commands, as the shanty man sprints toward him. The agent throws his forearm forward, trying to counter the slight man and his flimsy advance, and receives a voracious bite in return. The shanty man continues to hungrily bite into the agent's forearm.

"Don't shoot!" Natal shouts.

Two shots collapse the homeless man.

"Stop her!" Natal hears while running toward the scene. Three agents throw their bodies in front of her.

"Stand aside!" she yells.

"You may be in charge of this operation, but you are not in charge of this scene, or these men, any longer. Please leave this to me, commander."

The authoritative voice belongs to a Blue Jacket a couple yards from the scene. He clasps his hands behind his back, and receives Natal's restrained scowl without reciprocation. She returns to her car, leaving the scene behind. "Move out!" she orders, before entering her vehicle.

The long and winding road is a transparent thing. The journey can be dreamt, imagined, but not sensed, until it transpires. And from a certain vantage point, it can appear infinite, a never-ending story consisting of an amalgam of varied plot twists and turns, those slings and arrows of any fortune.

Some can focus on the first, then the second, then third, connecting a series of intentioned, and even unintentional, events, into a continuous stream, metamorphosing twist and turn to ebb and flow. For others, the transparency converges with the infinite and produces only the inevitability of certainty, an eternity of trivialities, and a forever of nothing.

Something is what Gabriel hoped for, anything, some flavor to relieve his tongue of ash. Something is what Gabriel hoped for yesterday, the day before, and every day previous, but not today. Today, Gabriel has resigned himself to nothing. Today he has chosen life without purpose, and he is lost to the consequences of his decision.

Walking through the hallway with quiet contempt existent in his dark, brooding eyes, he is consumed by the various counts running simultaneously in his mind. Foremost, the counting of his steps ticks along with every plant of his heel. He had also chosen black shoes today. Being a basic form of apparel, and therefore commonly occurring, he deemed them a suitable second focus to allow him to escape the trappings of his mind. Then there is the yellow nail polish. Counting only his 567th step of the day, he sat in his seat, and looked over to see two hands resting on respective thighs, each nail outfitted with a new coat of yellow nail polish. A rare and novel find, Gabriel was surprised to be at three by midday. His counts are only intended as a distraction for his mind. He never investigates too hard, only tabulating when items come to his attention. And, although he incessantly questions himself, his counts are never off.

He stops at his locker, having successfully avoided all the eyes thirsty for his attention and the gestures that intend to capture it. He opens the locker, slowly, methodically, because Gabriel no longer considers time. He has decided that the way it wraps around him, weaving in and out, casts the sole linear conception of it useless. No, he will weave in and out; he will acknowledge a fuller understanding, the temporal spectrum will—

"Are you crazy, boy?"

Gabriel swivels his head. Alohi stands directly behind him, as buoyant as ever and close enough to render his personal space now theirs. Gabriel's tired eyes only stare.

"You're just gonna leave me like that? You crazy?" she asks, in a feigned huff with a flirtatious smile.

"You just noticed?" Gabriel replies coolly.

Alohi's face loses humor and gains pallor as she meets the direct gaze of his sharp, lost eyes, and becomes lost with him.

"What's wrong with you? Why won't you let me like you? I know about all the girls you get around with. How are they . . . why are they better than me?"

"You think you'd like living in my delusion, huh."

"What?" Alohi responds, shaking her head.

"You don't know me," Gabriel says quietly.

"Why don't you give me a chance to?"

"You don't know me," he repeats.

"You don't feel anything between us?" she asks earnestly.

"You don't know me!" Gabriel shouts, with such ferocity that he stalls the busy hallway. They are now the center of attention, the life of the drab and dim hallway with its dirty trampled floor and dull green walls.

"What going on here?" the security guard asks, cutting through the silence as he appears at Gabriel and Alohi's side. He looks first to her face, and catches the pure shock and faint sadness there as she still looks to Gabriel. He turns to Gabriel with an intensity that is immediately overtaken by a solemn face with tired but soldering eyes. The triangle is frozen.

"Did you hear me? What's going on?" the security guard tries once more, attempting to impose every ounce of his tall, husky, native frame on the youth, who continue to stare at each other.

"Nothing. Nothing's going on," Alohi replies soberly and dismissively, before shaking her head and quickly walking away.

The security guard continues to look to Gabriel, trying to transmit a warning. Gabriel looks back, and then turns to open his locker. The guard flashes his anger before shaking his head also. He turns to the multitude that still stands captivated. His look is all that is needed to get them mobile once more.

Something is what Gabriel hoped for but could never see, no matter how plainly it presented itself. Today, he has chosen to resign himself to nothing. Today, he has chosen life without purpose. And so, he is lost to the consequences of that decision.

Ten

"I don't know."

"You don't know?"

"I don't know," Charles reiterates. He sits, sunken into the autumn orange couch in the living room of the large cabin, as he attempts to offload more than physical weight. His entire body lies limp; his head nestles into the sofa back, and his eyes search for nothing in the same spot on the ceiling.

"Spinning a bit out of control for you?" Mr. Grey inquires.

"A bit," Charles answers.

"Was there a plan?"

"There was, never really launched. Improvising, if you know what I mean," Charles replies.

"I can see. I uh, I've read up on you. You've been military for a long time, even Covert Operations for years. A solid record, trusted in the field, everything I've read about you has been practically eulogistic. I won't pretend to know you, but it seems a bit out of character. What happened on that train platform?"

". . . Honestly? I'm still questioning that myself. I just couldn't take . . . I just didn't know anymore . . . didn't know anything at that moment. There was a basic understanding of what would happen to him—nothing good—and then, after that, nothing. Nothing was real, nothing made sense. I reacted. Couldn't tell you to what, to that nothing maybe. He told me recently he hasn't felt real in a long time. Maybe I was . . . fighting against that nothing," Charles finishes, and his eyes find another spot on the ceiling.

"Can I ask how you got to this Island?"

Charles' head lowers. "Why do you ask?"

"I'm just interested," Mr. Grey answers awkwardly, aware of and uncomfortable with the fact that he is being examined.

"I was recruited," Charles offers, his attention still attuned to Mr. Grey. "Recruited by LE."

"So you just went from military to private police?"

"Something tells me that you know this story," Charles says, with a hint of suspicion.

"I'm not sure if Anon is the all-seeing-eye, but I'm certainly not," Mr. Grey answers, attempting to reassure.

"I was in a coma, seven months, after I was thrown by an explosion," Charles offers.

"IED?"

"Rocket. No major injuries. I was lucky—brain shut off—but still, I was lucky. Lucky again to wake up. When I did, docs advised against strenuous activity, advised against service, advised against everything I had done my whole life. I was an orphan, as a kid, and not the type that had a lot of friends . . . or any, really. The military gave me identity, you know? I was lost for a while, down for a while, never really had anyone for support.

"One day I get a call, a rep from LE, telling me they could

111

use me, must've somehow sniffed out my service records. A week later he's sitting in my apartment telling me the job isn't too strenuous, good pay, good location. He left a card, kept checking up, a call here, call there. Eventually I got tired of sitting, thinking, drinking. I thought the personal attention was a bit strange, but I always had a good feeling about it. I signed up.

"You know I always had a problem with the bullshit. I was always a bit subversive. I had a skill, though. I could bury it, get the job done. It's a lot harder without those flowery ideals like God and Country, though. You never feel comfortable hiding behind all the actually good reasons. Maybe they feel too sacred."

"It sounds like you're made of stuff that's pretty unique. From the outside, I couldn't say you have many options . . . is he always that loud?" Mr. Grey asks, in reference to the engineer whose body has fallen limp on a separate couch to Charles' right. His head leans awkwardly after falling asleep upright and his snores rumble.

"We've had to work on keeping him quiet at night. He's an interesting guy," Charles answers apathetically.

"Good thing for insulation. Well, I can offer you this place three more days, max."

"It'd be appreciated."

"No worries. It's a small island though, and it only gets smaller. You got a way out of here?"

"I'm pretty resourceful."

"I bet. And what about him?"

"I'm working on it."

"Yeah. Good luck with that," Mr. Grey replies. He

examines the unconscious engineer in his state of restful innocence. He appears blissfully lost and blithely contented to rest his constantly lost, imploring eyes and give himself up to whichever reality he now resides. "There is a way," he continues. "I've skimmed through that drive. The basic way it's organized, the files I've seen, there are things that are indicting, nothing damning. I'll keep looking, so will Anon. There might be something we can work with, but I wouldn't be surprised if there isn't much.

"But without anything substantial, it'll all get awash in conspiracy theorizing, too much money, influence on that side. Correspondence has left some trails we can wiggle our way into, but I can't promise anything except that it's going to take a while." Charles absorbs the information while barely blinking.

"And, no matter what we crack, whatever info we throw up will be disputed, assaulted. But if we had hard evidence . . ."

"What're you saying?" Charles asks, sitting up.

"It seems Anon has thought about your particular situation. 'Anon will always help a friend.' I'm sure it's one of the first messages they exchanged with you. They think they've found a mutually beneficial proposition for someone with your background."

"Just tell it to me plain, Grey."

"They want you to hack the Defense Ministry."

"Isn't that what you all are trying to do? I think you're much more qualified."

"Physically hack."

"You want me to commit a B&E? I asked for the plain version. For what?"

"Evidence. The Defense Ministry is intended to defend

against all crime, including property and intellectual theft."

"And?"

"Not only do they have a room full of hackers actively fighting system threats, all pertinent documents are housed in the Ministry's Documents and Records department, which can be better described as a digital library."

"And you think they've got some fucked-up shit hiding in there?"

"I know they do."

"You're not exactly living in a tent. Who are you, Grey? Anyone that goes by a name like that must've had a pretty colorful life at some point."

Mr. Grey clenches his jaw and contemplates. His eyes, which are the color of a dark ocean, are deep, as if they're wells to another world. His face is distinguished, attractive in a classic sense, but obscured by a haggardness complimented by his graying hair. His facial hair, which retains its natural brown hue, is untrimmed, and his lean body imprints him as a man in his late thirties, subtracting substantially from his forty-eight years.

"Full disclosure? For the sake of what I'm asking you, I'm a doctor. Well, was a doctor, a neuroscientist. Their scientist, for years I worked with LE. Brain augmentation, that's the best description I can give you of my work."

"Weird science."

"Weird science. Illegal science, a good amount of disgusting science."

"Examples?"

"Some demons are best dug up by others," Grey says with a heavy voice.

"Fuck you! Fuck you motherfucker! I'll fucking gut you, you piece of shit!" They both turn to see the unconscious, but animated, engineer, screaming in a reality his mind has conjured, only to settle back into his rumbling.

"What the—?" Grey asks.

"He's actually gotten a lot better," Charles responds. "So I take it this is redemption, restitution?"

"Aren't I allowed to try?"

The question lingers.

"What happened? Why the change of heart?" Charles asks.

"It wasn't my heart that changed, it was my mind. I always felt it was wrong, but what we were doing . . . what we did, it hadn't been done that way. We weren't opening Pandora's Box; we were taking it apart and putting it back together. I was a kid in a candy shop. When I came down from my sugar high, when I finally took my shades off, I looked around that lab and was horrified, completely disgusted.

"I was a wreck for a while, going nuts, coming apart and trying not to show it. I was suicidal, homicidal, derailed, lost nearly 20 pounds in two months. I couldn't eat. Every day, I looked sicker. Every day, on every side, there was more concern, caution, suspicion.

"One day, I just didn't show. It was a Monday. The weekend before I bought every ticket I could off this island. Some flight records were fudged; by the airline system logs, I checked into every one. I never left the island. Three days later, Anon leaked some videos that you've probably seen. I'm a whistleblower, whatever that's worth. The videos, documents, everything, pretty much excoriated from existence, all just a sideshow in the end. I thought I could solve the puzzle, understand the brain . . ."

"The path to hell . . ."

"Was paved by me . . ."

"How did you get to the camp?"

"I was already there. I make frequent trips. I'm a supply contact, among other things. I've been there for a few days, waiting to extract you, actually. You should know you're on the priority list. Anon believes there's a place for you."

"And this cabin?" Charles asks without wavering.

"Was for sale and purchased by a wealthy European businessman. Certain kinds of money aren't questioned on this island. Look, it's a lot to ask, but where do you go from here? With hard evidence, I'm not going to try to divine your chances, but you'll have one."

"Or, I'll become an unknown martyr."

"Welcome to Anon."

Charles sinks back into the sofa, this time shutting his eyes. "Okay. I'll be your agent of redemption. I'll do it. I just have one more question."

"What?"

"I understand this is a collective, but there's obviously someones or somethings behind all this. Who . . . what is Anon?"

"What I do know is that they can do things that give me hope. But if I knew what Anon was that would defeat the purpose of the pseudonym, wouldn't it?"

Charles smiles briefly with eyes still shut, cueing the doctor to get up. "You're friend seems to be doing something right. It'll be dark soon. You might want to catch up on some sleep."

116

"Doc," Charles says, "I just need one favor. I need an Anon message sent."

"You got it," the doctor responds as he heads to the door. "And Mike, thanks for being my confessor," he says at the doorway.

"It's good to get it out," Charles replies, "but at some point, you really got to let it in."

"Believe me, I'm trying."

The doctor leaves Charles to rest, but Charles knows sleep is only a dream. With his eyes closed, he enjoys the daydream.

Eight-o'six, the digital clock projects the time upward into thin air. Professor Campman lies on his side on the bed. A stack of papers sprinkled with red ink separate him from his wife, who lies on her side facing him. *Yellow Blossoms* is the title she holds in her hand, and her fingers are strategically embedded between pages. His concerned and imploring eyes now make her crease an edge of a page and lay the book down on his pages.

"So that's why you've been acting so funny these last two days? That's why you were so spooked at Adam's dinner the other night."

"Stella, I can't say I haven't been freaked out before, but . . . that was just crazy."

"You sure you haven't just been working too hard? You haven't really had a break in schedule for a while." His strained eyes are the answer she receives. "Then honey, what do you think it means?"

"I don't know, Estelle."

"Estelle? Now I know you're serious."

Campman cracks a smile. "I am serious about this, Stella."

"I know, I know, I'm hearing you. What do you want to do about it?"

"I don't know. I just had to tell someone. I mean, realistically, what can I do?" Campman asks. Worry is faintly present on his middle-aged face which still retains its boyish charm.

"You can file a report."

"Right, tell the spooks that they're spooking me out."

"Don't be such a conspiracy theorist."

"What if I'm right?"

"What if you are? Does it make anything worse? And if it's some deranged psycho, or even a fan, then what?"

"I know you're right, but I just feel like there's something more to it."

"You just said it; 'what can you do?' At least this is something. Can you promise me you'll file a report?"

"Are you really going to pull that card?"

"Promise me . . . please."

"Alright. Alright. You were born knowing how to get what you want, huh?"

"Just from you." She plants a kiss on his cheek.

"So I'm just a sucker."

"Yep, my sucker," she replies before edging over to the other side of the mattress and standing. He watches her get up and admires her form as her nightgown, a converted sundress, cascades down her slender body. The thin cotton hugs her elegant figure, as it stretches slightly from the small of

118

her back, over her buttocks, and falls down, ending just above her knees.

She turns, exposing her left side. Her breast fills out the dress amply and her nipple pokes out, erect.

"I feel like a shower," she says. Her plump lips defy their thin outline. Her high cheekbones lead to large eyes with long lashes, outlined by light crow's feet, the only real sign of aging on a face that his mother affectionately described as 'handsome pretty.'

"Keep me company?" she asks as she lets the dress fall and walks to the adjacent bathroom, leaving the door open and disappearing to the left.

"How's the Museum treating you?" he asks as he grabs his papers, letting the book slide down, and reflecting on how lucky he is.

"A bit stressfully. We have a new exhibit coming from a collective in British Columbia. The logistics are always consuming. I can't believe I haven't told you about it, it's been too long since we really talked."

'Economic theory,' he thinks with a sigh before putting his papers and red pen back down, and lying flat. "We're busy people."

"I hope it's not a trend," he hears over the shower.

He learned the hard way never to take the bait, not to indulge these entreaties into "penetrating" conversation. "What type of art is it?"

"Paintings, a collection of artists from BC. It's actually pretty interesting." She yells over the rushing water. "A local post-impressionist take on the modern idea of Canadian art. Kind of like Van Goghing twenty first century style, if that

119

makes any sense. It's definitely . . ."

Campman's phone rings on the bedside dresser. He picks it up after seeing the name.

"Dean Pierce, how are you?"

"Well, professor. Thank you for inquiring. And yourself?"

"Perty dang good, I gotta say," he replies ironically. He couldn't resist presenting a stark contrast to the dean's formality, sometimes diving close to the buffoonish. Knowing the adroit but understanding character of the man, he hoped he was in on the joke.

"Good to hear. Sincerest apologies on the timing of my call, but certain things have come to my attention that I believe require an ecumenical and mutually agreeable approach to their rectification."

"May I ask what these things are, dean?"

"I believe this to be an unsuitable medium to expound upon, or rather discuss, these pertinent discoveries. I've called to set up a meeting. This matter is pressing and so I would ask your favor in acquiescing to my request for fastidious conference."

"How soon?"

"In three days' time I'll be back, I've reorganized my schedule and will be able to accommodate you at three-thirty in the afternoon. I understand you have a small break within that window. Is this adequate and plausible timing?"

'Do I really have a choice?' "Yes, Dean Pierce, sounds good."

"Good to hear. Thank you for your sanctimonious disposition, and again, apologies for the timing."

"No problem, dean."

"Best regards to your wife and family. Good night, professor."

"Good night."

The line goes dead. Campman wonders about the strange urgency and severity in the dean's tone. He knew Pierce was capable of this, but had never experienced it himself.

"Are you asleep?" Estelle asks half-jokingly, in the doorway of the bathroom. She stands naked, wet, and dripping, and approaches while drying herself off in sections. "Who was that?" she asks, registering his expression.

"Just the dean," Campman answers, still puzzled.

"Is everything alright?" she asks, with genuine concern.

He looks her over slowly. He was surprised that after years, his mind never delved into insecurity over her stature, even though she stood a full two inches over him. Now she overwhelms his senses.

She sees him concentrating on her round buoyancy, her long nipples peak above large areolas. She looks down. "I guess I'm cold," she says.

Campman laughs, the previous tenseness now easing with the flight of comprehensive thought. "You look a little cold. Can I warm you up over here?" She begins to climb onto the bed. "You always know how to get what you want, huh?"

"Just from you." She kisses him, pressing her softness against him.

Eleven

Gabriel cracks his bedroom door ajar, hearing the front door close in the process. The light flicks on.

"Hey, Ma," he says softly.

"Gabriel? What are you doing awake?" she asks, as he leaves his room, shutting the door securely behind him. It's 1:30 in the morning!"

"You're home late."

"I had to stay late today. Are you ok? Have you been throwing up?"

"No."

"Are the headaches too bad? Are you taking your medicine? Gabriel, you need to take your medicine."

"No, Ma, really. I just want to talk."

"Gabriel, you know I have to sleep. I have to work in a couple hours. Have you been going to school?"

"Two or three days a week."

"Okay, try to do more if you can, alright," she says. "Have you been doing your homework, are they still emailing it?" He nods. "You still work at the little surf shop?" He nods. "Is it okay?"

"It's good, relaxing."

"Good, that's good. You keep going outside, alright? Surf, skate, alright? If it helps, yeah? As long as you're safe," she says, now nodding herself.

"Yeah," he replies, instinctually nodding in return. "What you reading now?" he asks, gesturing toward the book in her hand.

"It's just a book about Polynesian settlement here. I know how you like Hawaiian history; I'll give it to you when I'm done. I'll leave it outside your door." Gabriel purses his lips. "You know I love you, Gabriel. You know, right?"

"Yeah, Ma."

"You gonna do better than you did last time in school, yeah?"

"I got all A's."

"You gonna do better next time, yeah?"

"Yeah."

"Alright, it's almost been three months; don't forget our appointment with the specialist next week. We're going to find out what it is and make it go away, alright," she affirms, resting her hand against his cheek. Gabriel manages a smile.

She gives him a hug and wraps her arms around him, sinking into his larger body as if he were her protector. He wraps his arms gently around her head.

"You know I love you, right?"

"Yeah, Ma, I love you too. Get some sleep," he advises, loosening his grip.

"Yeah, I have to," she agrees, leaving the embrace.

"I'll turn off the light."

"Thank you, baby." She walks through the small living

room, into the kitchen, and disappears in the darkness. Gabriel hears a door open and close. He relieves his eyes of light and walks back to his room in darkness.

Once inside, he walks to his dresser and tosses another pill into his mouth, swallowing without liquid. His eyes are wet with perspiration that he wipes away. He sits down at the foot of his bed and then lies on his side. His body begins to curl, past fetal, into a ball. He raises his hands to his temples. He can only imagine blades slicing through grey matter as he is no longer able to abate the pain. His eyes moisten and he attempts to blink them dry. His jaw clenches tighter and tighter as he feels his enamel bulge.

The branches alternate between a flutter and a sway in the stiff wind. Light debris breezes by Charles on occasion, jarred loose by the rapid airflow. He makes out a figure approaching through the trunks of the thick palms. Casually, Natal meanders through nature. Neither wavers from eye contact.

"You always loved this place," he says, outlining her face, trying to capture a mental image.

"I thought we both did." A non-physical exhaustion oozes from her, even dwelling in her wired eyes, which never stray from him.

"I still do. I remember you telling me that when you were a kid, they never kept up the palms section."

"Is that why you chose it?"

"You always seemed to like it here . . . how'd they explain the Fifth Floor?"

"Updated security clearances, promotions, transfers."

"Sounds about right."

"I think we're past the point of pleasant conversation."

"Unfortunately, that's all I had in mind."

A standoff.

"Why do you think I won't arrest you?"

"I don't . . ."

Silence.

"What—do you want! The words come out in an unexpected shrill shout, leaving Natal wild-eyed and fuming.

Charles is unable to move, unable to take his eyes from her. ". . . To say goodbye."

"Oh, so you're sentimental now?" she asks, trying to calm her heaving chest. The wind doesn't help, offering gusts of swirling air to her lungs. He can only look. Tears breach her lids and trail down her angry face. "Why? Why did you do this?" she asks, shaking her head.

He lowers his head, acquiescing, forfeiting. "I'm sorry," he says in his baritone. Slowly he raises his head, grief inhabits his expression. "I always admired . . . loved you, because you believed in what a thing stood for, not what it was. You believed in what it stood for, and you fought to make it what it should be. I always have to poke holes to see if it holds water." He stops, and waits for judgment.

"You never understood. You're what I believe in. You're all I believe in anymore." The wind dries the last of her tears, leaving streaks on her face.

"Give me time; I can make sense of this," he says, almost pleading.

"Take me with you."

"What?"

"Take me with you," she repeats.

"You know I can't do that."

"Why not? You don't trust me?"

"No. What? What are you saying, Gwen?"

"I can't trust the Ministry anymore, I can't—"

"Shhh," Charles whispers, placing his finger to her mouth. "Take cover." Slowly he kneels and guides her down. He points to the tree beside her and follows her to shelter.

"Did you tell anyone?"

She shakes her head. He wets his thumb and wipes away the streaks on her face. She smiles all the while, and then turns to her side of the large palm. They both look to the same direction.

In the brush, a twig gently snaps. "Might be tracked, we have to go." Charles says.

"Run on three," she says without turning. "Meet you at the guava."

"I won't leave without you. One . . . two . . ."

They both book it, running in opposite directions, weaving between the large palms, and are suddenly affronted with a barrage of shots bursting from what sounds like one weapon. They take cover and turn to see Jezequel duck behind an African palm after letting off several shots in Charles' direction.

Weapons immediately become ready. Charles looks to Natal, who squats behind the huge trunk of a palm with firearm in hand. Shots lodge into his natural cover as he watches Natal return fire.

The air dances on the hot hazy day. The palms that tower over them are bastions of the tropical condition, but fail to alleviate the tension.

Natal gives the signal to separate, and Charles immediately shakes his head. She tries again and once more encounters opposition. She is right, he knows. They soon may be surrounded by surveillance, authority, captivity. She repeats the order and motions that she will move out. Finally he overrides emotion, and assents with several nods. She holds up her index finger.

"You always seemed like the type that wanted to be in a shootout," Charles shouts.

She raises her middle finger. "You seem like the type that would call this a firefi . . ."

With her ring finger raised, they book it, pelting the thick trunk Jezequel is ensconced behind with bullets, and then sprinting. Charles, who is headed for a thicket of bushes, hears bullets directed elsewhere. Turning, he sees Jezequel targeting Natal, and immediately leans against a trunk and attempts to provide cover.

In vain, he attempts to direct shots through the mass of palms occupying this section of the arboretum. With no available shot, he runs toward her, looking for an angle, and watches as Natal tries to make it to the edge of the slope that angles downward through the Asian palms.

Natal nears the edge of the slope. She leans against a trunk and lets off shots, attempting to buck the pressure. Jezequel, in parallel pursuit, puts his back to a trunk. He rolls around to the other side, and aims at Natal, who runs as low as possible looking to dive down the steep slope. The sun favors her, its light flooding Jezequel's eyes as he fires off three shots.

Charles immediately runs in her direction after hearing a

low cry and watching her tumble down and out of sight. He's greeted by shots and fires back, stopping and taking cover.

"I knew you'd come back for that bitch," Jezequel screams maniacally. "To think I looked up to you, the great fucking Mike Charles! Now everyone can see who you really are."

Charles leaves cover, making his way quickly and quietly. Jezequel peeks from his refuge to see Charles sprinting to a tree ten yards out. Charles aims, but doesn't fire as he darts behind the tree and avoids shots.

Lying flat, Charles pokes out the edge of the palm, forcing Jezequel to retreat. Charles rises, and sprints toward the enemy encampment.

Jezequel hears the soft, rapid steps, peeks again from his kneeling position, and tucks his head back, having seen Charles with gun drawn running towards him. Two bullets whiz by Jezequel and burrow into the dirt.

With his gun held before him, Jezequel rolls around the right side of the trunk and pulls the trigger as his hand is batted away, letting off a shot to nowhere. Charles, whose back rests against the tree, grabs Jezequel's gun-filled right hand with his left. Charles is unable to aim with his own right hand before Jezequel grabs his arm, pulling it to Jezequel's own side. Registering Charles' large brow, Jezequel turns his back to him, gaining leverage. With his left arm holding Charles' right by Jezequel's own right hip, Jezequel pulls back his right elbow, connecting with Charles' cheek and loosening Charles' grip on his arm.

Jezequel attempts to pull his shooting arm down. Charles releases his own weapon, raises his arm under the pit of Jezequel's shooting arm, and grabs his wrist. Swiftly, he releases, and slides his left arm to Jezequel's throat. Jezequel tries too late to use his chin as guard, as Charles squeezes the air from him.

Falling to his back, Charles holds the shooting arm above his own head, twisting and applying pressure to Jezequel's wrist, while pushing upward on the neck. Charles wraps his left leg around Jezequel's torso, sun rays shine down on them and the blue sky above steadies Charles' mind.

Jezequel, being stretched as if racked, attempts to thrash about, trying to escape the improvised blood choke. His muscles, deprived of oxygen, weaken as he releases his gun. Charles releases the wrist, smacking the gun away, and then presses firmly against the back of Jezequel's head. With the figure four firmly in place, Jezequel feels himself fading. He frantically searches for Charles' gun with his free hand, then with seemingly his last flash of consciousness, lifts his right leg, pulling a large hunting knife from a slit in his boot.

Once unsheathed, the glint from the blade shines into Charles' eyes. Jezequel weakly attempts to settle the knife into Charles' thigh. Charles kicks at the hand and hilt, removes his lock on Jezequel's life, and putting his feet to Jezequel's shoulders, rolls away.

Before Charles can retrieve a weapon, Jezequel pops up. With the eyes of a wounded animal and the taste of second life fresh on his tongue, he charges Charles with the blade. Charles dodges a swipe to his neck. Jezequel brings the knife down and up again. Charles pulls back and the blade slices his right breast. Charles pushes forward before Jezequel can bring the blade down again, grabs his arm and connects with a sharp hook to Jezequel's jaw. Holding his arm firmly, Charles pulls Jezequel to him once more, and again connects, this time to his face, leaving Jezequel's mouth open and bloody.

Jezequel's hand opens, letting the blade drop, and his body slumps, leaving him kneeling. Charles releases his hand, allowing Jezequel to fall to his back with his legs crooked below him and his arms stretched to either side.

Charles grabs the knife and places his knee on Jezequel's stomach. "You want to try to cut into my heart?" he says, as he sinks the knife into Jezequel's chest. His hand smothers a moan already obscured by gargling. Charles' body jerks as he twists the knife and he is up and running before life is extinguished from the eyes.

Charles flies down the shallow decline, reaching Natal, who kneels beside a tree. "Gwen, babe, you alright?" He dashes to her front, and his face immediately drops as he sees the blood and hole in the side of her torso.

"Babe, no, baby, Gwen, you alright? Can you move?" he asks over her wheezing. His face is frantic and their eyes are locked as he watches her labor for breath.

"He must've . . ." she starts, and then sucks in deep.

"Don't talk, don't talk," Charles says in desperation.

"Suspicious," she finishes. "I sent them away."

"I can carry you, here."

"No," Natal says, stalling Charles, whose arms are nearly around her. Her wheezing slows in speed and severity. "You have to go."

"You know I can't, Gwen . . ." Words are lost; he can't find any as he watches her fight for air. Her breath slows still.

"Promise me you'll . . ." Her eyes are locked on his, looking deep into him, as she stops.

"Gwen!" he hollers, putting his hands to her shoulders. "Gwen," he tries, giving her a soft shake. Tears trickle down his face. "Gwen," he says one last time. Silence reigns. He buries his head in her chest and clutches her tightly. He emerges from her breast, his face aghast. He allows himself one last look before gently laying her down. He kisses her forehead, stands, and runs downhill. He makes it through thicket and bush to the trail, where he crosses to the Economy Zone. Past papaya and star fruit, he runs to a stream that he crosses over to Manoa Falls.

Twelve

Her hips sway from side to side as she embellishes her femininity. They frame two long halves of a slender, toned body. The cheeks of her butt hang from cut-out shorts that barely extend below her waist, giving way to the fishnet that sections diamonds out of her legs.

With each step, she extends her legs to their full length and succeeds that with a slight dip on red heels, the same color as her lipstick. She moves as if awaiting a celebration of her body, and walks among others who await and receive the same. She walks and strolls, forth and back, down Kuhio Avenue, with its neon gilt; lights dance upon every sidewalk.

A block away, Kalakaua Avenue is drowned in gold and white light, offering the idea of class and the reality of luxury to those able and willing to pay for it. But here, Kuhio only offers uncertainty amidst the backdrop and possibility of pleasure. This is night in Waikiki, the massive hotels and developments enveloping all, creating a fishbowl of hedonistic stimulation.

"Pay to play," Mike pontificates as he sits in the driver's seat. He calls out to the long-legged beauty with his index finger.

"Got friends?"

"Of course," she says as she lowers her head to the window, making sure to breach the enclosure.

"You think you can squeeze four of them in this truck?"

"Depends on what we're doing in there."

"I like the mouth on you," he replies, as he looks up and down her face, from her narrow eyes, to her tan skin and glossy lips. "Round up some friends, let's go."

She looks at him, then at the beat-up SUV he occupies. He hands her a hundred, and gives her a smile after pocketing the large wad of cash it came from. "I'll make it worth your time."

She smiles back. It takes her less than a minute to fill his van. "You're the least creepy and the best looking," was the line the doctor used to solicit Mike for this task. He looks to the lanky beauty to his right, and smiles once again. She smiles back as they drive down the Avenue, past sailors, past lady boys who actively proposition, past throngs, and glamour with glitz. He drives in silence, keeping his empty eyes on the road ahead.

The hotel clerk stares at the scantily and suggestively clad women clustered together in the lobby as the doctor slips him cash. They look oxymoronic. Their ornate and revealing guises offset the elegance of the lobby.

"Thanks for the hospitality," the doctor says, and turns to follow the rest into the elevator. They make it to their room on the seventh floor and enter a spacious and luxurious room carpeted in burgundy.

The four men immediately spread out, getting acclimated to

their surroundings.

"We've got about forty-five minutes left," the doctor whispers to Charles.

"You good to go?" Charles primes.

"Better be. You?"

Charles nods.

"I'll be back," the doctor says before turning. "Jim," he says to a husky man in their party, "I'll be back."

"Ladies, will you accompany me?" The doctor says to the four women who immediately line up. Together, the group departs.

Charles looks at the engineer who sits on the couch, observing the faint seediness in his face and realizing that it will actually come in handy.

"I'm going, you good?"

The engineer nods.

Charles crosses the room and walks into the spare bedroom. Once there, he grabs a chair, walks to the large walk-in closet, and sits inside, going over the plan in his head . . .

. . . "He's from Invision," the doctor says.

"Communications? What's the trip for?" Charles asks.

"A development contract, they're laying down infrastructure soon. He's in town to sign papers. There's a lot of high-profile people in and out the ministry for all types of activity, but this guy's our in."

"Why so?"

"Well, basic procedure is security detail from the airport, nothing extravagant, four men, PD, discreet. They don't want

134

to call attention."

"I know. The men love those jobs, easy, pays better than traffic duty."

The Doc laughs. "Well, this guy, he's a philanderous one. All we do is separate him from his detail, we become his detail, and we're in. All we need are some guys—I'll take care of that—and some women that'll convince his libido."

"You all don't appear to be underfunded." Charles remarks.

The doctor laughs again. "Cash is still king and sometimes ATMs hiccup. We can blind the hotel, say an hour, we won't have to worry about surveillance."

"Sounds good, but I've done the detail. Two in, two out, and the two in escort until he's where he needs to be and back. There's no leeway."

"I've gotten you blueprints, security procedures, pass-codes shuffle. I've got no other assistance on the inside. I can get you in. I wouldn't know what to do in there. I'm banking on the fact that you do. This is what I can do; it's up to you if you want to accept it."

"I've been in there, it's a fortress. Any in is good, just have to be a bit creative with this one. Give me a little time and I'll figure it out."

"We go in two days, you got 'til then."

"I don't have much time as it is. Two days . . .

. . . Sitting in the mahogany chair inside the closet, Charles hears the blaring music emanating from the living room, which barely seeps through the thick walls.

Walking down the hall, the doctor, accompanied by his flock of peacocks, stops in front of room 719. He rings the bell.

135

"Who's there?" asks a husky voice from inside.

"Front Desk," the doctor replies, steadying his face in front of the peephole.

"What is it?"

"Package."

"Leave it at the door."

"I have instructions to hand deliver," the doctor replies. He overhears a soft, indecipherable, verbal exchange.

"Open the door . . . just open the door," the doctor hears as someone raises his voice.

The door opens to reveal the VP of the Korean company, a taller man, well built, with a pretty-boy face, standing behind three men in well-tailored suits, with guns in hand. An officer holds the door open. Three others are seated at a table farther back. Each holds cards in their hands, and a pile of cards lies between them.

"What is it?" the VP asks in a calm and eloquent voice.

"A gift," the doctor responds, motioning to his right.

Every eye in the room is captivated by the tall tan creature who enters the room and stands before them. The VP watches her as if he is the first to discover some rare, exotic species.

"Come here," he says, motioning her forward with an open hand. She consents, walking in her usual elongated step, with no diminishing confidence. The three suited men part.

She stands before the man who beckoned her. As he looks into her eyes, she notices his robe rise. With no hint of shame or embarrassment, he reaches for her head. Both hands trace her profile. Gently he glides from the back of her ears to her neck, then her shoulders. He goes down her arms, then up

136

the insides, where he moves to her ribcage. He squeezes slightly, and then runs his hands to her chest, from the collar bone down to her breasts, cupping each one before moving to her back. His hands trail from her shoulder blades, down to her backside, where he grabs each cheek. He moves to the front of her thighs, rubbing down each pants pocket, then moves to the button. He undoes the button of her hot pants, guiding them over her ass, exposing a pair of black panties. He lets them drop. Crouching, he maneuvers them away from each heel, as she picks up each leg. Standing slowly, he runs his hand up the back of her legs, while holding the bottoms, and inspecting her front intently. Standing erect again, he inspects the inside of the shorts briefly before tossing them across the room to the doctor.

"Who, may I ask, sent me such a fine gift?" the VP asks while holding her against him and staring at her face, from lips to eyes. She stares back.

"The Ministry. I have something for your detail as well," the doctor informs, as he motions for the other women who walk in and stand in front of him. "I have a separate room for them. I was told to relay a message: the entertainment and privacy are a gesture of goodwill."

The VP looks up after hearing the message. He looks at the women, then the officers.

"You all seem to be smart enough. Do you understand?"

They all affirm, some gesturing, some verbally, all with eyes fixed on the women.

"Don't worry, if she manages to drain me, you can each have a turn," the VP says to his own security, as he holds his hand out. "I can search you better in the bedroom," he says.

She takes his hand and follows . . .

. . . "A lot of mutual distrust is being broadcast through the grapevine," the doctor explains, addressing the congregated group of conspirators. "This contract is more like a royal marriage, and this detail is as much for protection as it is for efficiency and surveillance.

"He'll be escorted from the airport in the morning. Then there'll be a tour of the areas to be secured. An undercover agent will be embedded in the detail. One Blue Jacket to relay details, that's the only real threat to catch our scent. But our play is off the tension."

Seated in a chair before the four other men, the Doc looks amongst them as he speaks.

"Any idea which one?" Jim asks.

"No," the Doc answers. "No info on that."

"You can bet on the least vocal, but he'll be making the decisions," Charles chimes in. "It's rare for an agent and commander to work this detail, except for high-profile cases. I've done it. When they sneak a Blue Jacket in, the commander gets certain details. Our job is to maintain rank, keep order, but the agent's in charge. Shouldn't matter this time around, though."

"It *shouldn't* matter," the Doc reaffirms.

"This is going to happen no matter what. There won't be many people interested in changing it or dealing with the repercussions. The mark, he's an important cog, but just a cog. He also keeps his own security team, better than anything the Ministry will give him. He won't be worried about his safety.

"The ministries work efficiently. Timelines are important. If anything happens to delay this, other realities in the timeline are delayed. For this reason over any other, he'll have no freedom until business is done. This is how the ministries do business; security is more about control and observation. He'll be itching for the business trip to end and the pleasure one to begin, so he'll jump at the chance to start it early. We just have to give everyone else a reason to let him," the Doc concludes.

"It's all itinerated. Debrief once they return from the hotel, then watch in hour intervals from 11:00 pm. In between he's in the room, probably watching porn, sending smoke signals, and telegraphing Morse, while the men in black sit around the table shooting shit," Charles interjects.

"Nine to ten, that's our window," the Doc continues. "We deliver the package, along with a special message, then when . . .

. . . "I feel like waking those motherfuckers up. I know they're sleeping, I doubt either of those assholes can last this long. Man, you go, I'll keep watch. Fuck them pulling rank. If they say anything, tell them we're tired. They have a lot more to lose than us," one officer says to the other, after two hours and fifteen minutes of watch.

"Forget that, man, this is Ministry work. I'm getting paid well, I'm not messing this up for anything. You really want to, you go. I'll stay."

"Fuck man, you know I'm just talking shit," the first officer replies. "This is bullshit," he lets off once more before settling back into his chair.

Several minutes later he hears a beep. Looking at his radio display, he reads to himself and then animatedly repeats, 'Watch is over. Come join the fun, boys.' "They're telling us to join in man, let's go."

"Let me see that," the second officer no sooner asks before the message is before his eyes. "I got a wife, kids, I don't need that. You go."

"You really want to be the only guy that stays behind? You sure that's a good idea?"

'That's an order,' the message comes in with another beep.

"I'm going, man. You stay if you want."

"Alright, I'm coming."

Seven thirty-two is emblazoned in gold on the black door they stand before. Turning the knob, they open the door and are met with nothing, emptiness. The smell of fresh cigarette smoke wafts about. Only the doctor sits, alone, and centered on the sofa with arms spread. The men enter the room, shutting the door behind them.

"Door number two," the Doc explains as he waves his left hand to the second bedroom.

"We don't get no privacy?" queries the outspoken officer.

"Plenty of opportunity for that in there," the Doc replies.

The two men shuffle semi-confidently past the Doc and to the door. They open it. The officer in the doorway motions for his weapon, the one behind turns and is confronted by the Doc who fires the Taser in his hand. All sound is muffled by the music and muted by the heavy insulation.

Three-quarters of an hour later, Charles and Jim re-enter the living room. "Sleeping sound?" the Doc asks.

"In a cozy pile on the bed," Charles answers.

"At least they have underwear on," the Doc replies.

"That's what you think," Jim says.

Charles shakes his head and all four men, dressed in uniform, stand and look each other over. "A little baggy," Charles says to the engineer, "but we should all be good."

"Seven hours 'til go time," the Doc exclaims. "Everyone good?"

He looks to his right and the engineer gives a sheepish smile. The two men beside him nod aggressively. To his left is Charles, whose purposeful eyes dip as he gives a single nod. He grabs his helmet and retreats once more to his closet, where he waits out the sun.

A low beep marking eight in the morning wakes Charles from his slumber; he leaves his refuge, walks past the pile of bare bodies and into the living room, where the Doc and Jim sit talking.

"Twenty minutes, I'll wake up the rest," the Doc says. Charles nods as the Doc stands and exits.

"You comfortable with this?" Charles probes, once he and Jim are alone.

"I'm not sure that matters at this point," he responds.

"Just remember, when I leave that elevator, you grab him and go. Get out as quick as you can."

Twenty minutes later, with Charles at the head of the group, they knock on the door of room 719. The VP's security opens it to reveal the freshly attired VP sitting in wait. His left arm is wrapped around his new friend, who sits in a hotel robe and casually drapes one leg over him.

"There's been no contact with your prior security. Are they here?" Charles asks, standing in the doorway.

141

"I haven't seen them," the VP replies with a straight face.

"Do you have any idea what could have happened to them?"

The VP laughs jovially. "I hope nothing too bad . . . or good," he replies with a smirk.

Charles' head turns from the VP to his friend and back again. "There's no time for this. I have a man bringing the car around. We're going."

Thirteen

"I love you," Charles hears as he walks up the steps to the Ministry. Two voices repeat the phrase; their competing tones collide and vibrate in his head.

The mass of concrete steps and the glass that fronts the large building portray an intended grandness and impregnability. Charles walks to the right side of the VP, while Jim guards his opposing side. Both match his step, scaling step by step to open the double glass doors of the main entryway. Confidently crossing the floors of the lobby, with the sun pouring in from behind and casting their shadows onto the terrazzo they tread upon, they walk to the reception area where they are corralled into a single file by walk-thru detectors.

"Weapon, commander," a Blue Jacket requests at the head of the detectors. Charles offers his firearm, releasing the magazine and laying it along with his weapon flat on a metallic tray the agent points to. "Thank you," the Blue Jacket imparts, handing him a tag after inspecting the barrel of his pistol.

Unloading his duty belt onto a conveyor, Charles leads them through, passing by the security guard, one of three stationed behind each detector. On the other side, he retrieves and equips his gear and stops beside a reception desk.

"Hello." The voice coming from the tan woman sounds robotic. She indeed appears almost robotic with her hair wrapped and swirled tightly into a nest above her head, a head that sits poised upon the ballast that is her sturdy neck. Her rectangular glasses outline an idyllic face that remains motionless when she speaks. "What can I do for you?" she asks, pleasantly, but with no expression.

"Nuong," the VP says suggestively, elongating every syllable.

She registers instantly and turns to the screen. "10:30 am, Mr. Nuong, VP, Invision. Thank you, Mr. Nuong," she rifles off mechanically, and follows with a smile that threatens to crack her face. The metal turnstiles slide open and the party proceeds.

The soles of Nuong's shoes clatter against the floor as he and his escort rush to one of the numerous elevators before them. The third left of center offers them the privacy they seek. Nuong stares at the button after pressing it, impatiently trying to exert his will on the carriage. The door opens and the VP enters first with detail following. The roundure containing the number thirteen lights up after Nuong presses it. The elevator starts with a jolt and begins to ascend rapidly.

Charles quickly presses eight once the elevator blinks six, and smashes the small camera in the left corner of the carriage with his baton as the elevator stops.

"What are you doing, officer!" Jim shouts, reaching for his own weapon.

"Don't!" Charles screams, turning his baton to high and

144

waving it at Jim. He slides the baton from Jim's belt. Charles reaches for the lobby button when, suddenly, a blaring alarm sounds, demanding attention, and leaving Charles scrambling through the elevator door as it closes.

Charles checks his watch then takes a left outside the elevator, running down the corridor, streaming by the white, sterile walls. He dips low and takes the second right hard. A woman in dark garb, carrying a stack of files, hugs the wall as he runs to her.

"Open the door!" Charles screams at her. "The fucking door!" he screams again at the deer in headlights.

"No!" she yells back, sliding to the floor and balling up. He grabs her by the arm, hoists her up and thrusts her toward the door.

"I want your hand, not you," he says softly as he rests against the door.

Her face is flush as she inputs the code. She closes her eyes and presses her hand against the pad that juts out from the wall, opening them again when the door slams in her face.

The elevator begins to move, descending rapidly, breaking the confused silence of Jim and Nuong and replacing it with an expectant one. Down, down, down, they go, past the lobby to the third level of the basement.

They stop. The door slowly opens, and they face a veritable firing squad as a slew of guns are pointed in their direction.

"What is the other officer intending to do?" The agent at the front line of the firing squad questions.

"I don't know what's going on."

"Name and rank, officer."

"Anthony Barea, Lieutenant."

"One more time, officer, do you have any involvement in this?"

"I don't know what's going on." Jim retorts back as aggressively. "Goddammit!" he yells, falling to the floor after receiving a bullet in his leg for the answer.

"I'll only ask once more, do you have any involvement in this, officer?"

"I don't know shit." Jim yells at the barrel of the gun that is now pointed at his head. It responds with a single shot.

"You three, detain Mr. Nuong and clean this up. The rest of you come with me."

Charles finds himself in a bare, concrete room. He walks forward, through sliding glass doors, into a circular atrium. Looking up, he can see past the tinted glass roof, past the numerous stories of the Ministry of Defense, to the shaded morning sky. Two curved staircases flank him and lead up, until they meet in front of him and turn into a walkway that disappears beyond his sight. Columns separate seven lanes of tall shelving. Charles chooses the lane left of center, crouches, and makes his way as quickly as possible. He stops at a break in the shelves and rests in between two of them.

Ahead of him, the walkway above diverges at another circular area, and again turns into two staircases that lead down to a steel door, in front of which, is a lone, standing guard. Charles takes his phone from his pocket. He turns, still crouched, into the central lane and points his phone at the guard. A red light shines on the guard's cheek and trails along his face, finding his eye before he can fire at Charles.

146

"Agghh," he lets out a short cry as he falls to his knees with his hand to his eyes. "Thanks for the hack, Doc," Charles whispers to himself, returning to his initial lane and rushing through. Charles comes out into the open and softly sprints to the guard. His foot lands with a thud, the guard aims at him with head hung low, and shoots. The bullet misses Charles who is upon the guard with his next step, twisting and wrenching the weapon from his clutch.

He smacks the guard with the butt end of the weapon once, then twice, and then grabs his hand and places it to the console by the door. The door slides apart to reveal a lambent room. Charles blinks twice before entering.

The security chief reaches the door to the Digital Documents and Records Department. He depresses his hand on the pad and the door slides apart. "Fan out, groups of two. Clement, Atkins, with me," he says as he rushes forward, immediately moving towards the mainframes. There he finds Charles kneeling with his hands securely behind his head. "Lie flat," the security chief commands. Charles complies. "Detain him," the chief commands once more. "Couldn't find the exit?" he taunts.

"Never planned on leaving," Charles answers.

Extending his legs at a fevered clip, Campman tries his best to limit the extent of his tardiness. He is late; it is inevitable. The day had already stretched each hour to its productive potential, but the faculty dean's tone rang in his ears as he sprang toward the office.

Floating down the corridor, he catches a glimpse of the

university's symbol; the crown he never much cared for. It was oxymoronic, in his opinion, to his belief of the egalitarian ethos of education, an ethos that should be devoid of any totalitarian or dictatorial sentiment. And then, the university's emblem comes to his mind.

This emblem, it was the reason he chose this institution of higher education over all others. Since he first saw it, it was how he approached his profession every day. As he thought of the women whose students looked up at her, wanting her to educate them of the living world, he would envision his own students as babes. He always tried to move beyond relaying information, beyond expounding upon talent, drive, uniquity; he wanted to strip each one of their malice and guile, so that they could desire the sincerest milk of the world, as Peter had described, so they could grow.

He composes himself outside the office door. He turns the knob and opens the door; the carpeted reception area emanates warmth.

"Professor Campman, the dean is waiting for you," the receptionist greets.

He proceeds into the office. The dean sits, angled away from his desk, staring out the window. Campman has never seen the dean idle. He senses trouble. "Sorry I'm late." Campman says, trying not to sound excusatory.

"It's alright, professor," the dean replies. Casually swiveling in his chair, he rights himself in front of his desk. "As a herald of enlightenment, I presume your obligations are occasionally an encumbrance to your punctuality." His hair always grabs Campman's attention. Not only white, but bright, it always requires a significant mental effort for Campman not to stare.

He can't help but think of how it would be like to go through your twenties with grey hair, as he heard the dean had.

"Again, I thank you for such velocious conference. To plunge directly into the crux of the matter at hand, it has come to my attention that an appreciable number of your recent performances—or rather, public interactions and journalistic endeavors—contain pejorative and defamatory comments. These incidents are antithetical to this institution's beliefs, and the decorum we expect from its representatives. These assertions, of course, required investigation and adjudication at the previous assembly of our board, and it is within my province to inform you of those decisions."

"Am I in trouble, dean?" Campman asks quizzically.

"Professor, your publishings, numerous and highly regarded, and your capacity to attract an array of minds, prove you are a substantive asset to this institution. You have always been regarded as an enduring investment. A mutual intendment is best."

"Who did I defame?"

"Professor, based on the unofficial nature of this investigation and conversation, I believe details would only serve as a detriment to this colloquy."

"What did I say—when?" Campman asks, faintly defiant.

"Professor Campman, I hoped my predilection for a consentient conclusion would match your proclivity for the same."

"How about you talk to me like a person and tell me what you want, dean," Campman rifles, the ensnaring nature of the conversation now fueling him.

The dean bores through Campman with his eyes, his face

bunched into a peculiar expression of analyzation, an almost alien expression nearly extraneous to the situation and himself. "Although this institution is a fierce proponent of intellectual freedom, we are also an advocate of discretion. We require a broader and larger involvement in your editorial process."

"And what exactly would that involvement involve?"

"That question requires an intricate answer. This conversation is to determine how committed you are to finding out what that answer should be."

Campman can't help shaking his head. "You're trying to censor me. And what if I say 'fuck you.'"

"I would first question your choice and debasement of language. Then I would question your decision. No one is trying to censor you, professor, but again, you are a representative of this community."

"Is this for real? What makes you think I won't just pack up and go?"

"Feel free; certainly, you have that right. But I cannot ensure that this institution will be able to support you in any future endeavors, and I will, of course, need to be entirely forthcoming about your behavior while here."

"Are you threatening me?"

"Of course not, professor. Am I not allowed to be honest? And to be honest, we are the oldest institution of higher education in this state. Do you believe many other institutions will be willing, or able, to involve themselves with you? What you fail to understand is that they will receive the same pressure we have, but will be much less equipped to handle it."

"What? What pressure?" Campman feels those dark, penetrating eyes, once again.

"Professor, I never mistook you for naive or obtuse. You are an asset to this community, an intellectual, an award-winner, a draw. Tenure we can assure, even protection, until, and if, you decide to blaze your own trail. Best of luck, if you so choose. Education, though, is still a business, and we are beholden to that community as well. I can assure you it will be a cold world once you leave this comfort."

Campman's stomach drops; the lump in his throat begins to swell. "So this is a business, and I'm a commodity?" he manages hoarsely.

"An investment. We all exist temporally, professor, in relation to time and space. This is where we are now."

Campman lowers his eyes to the dean's desk. He mentally jousts with one idea, his mind turning it over and over. *Every crown has an emblem.*

It is mid-day. Gabriel sits and scans the two lines repeatedly.

Implant Serial #JS23

Type: PDAR Physics and Dynamic Anatomical Rendering

He finally breaks through the trance. His face slightly buried in the screen, he continues to virtually thumb through the pages, encountering documents laced with descriptive jargon. He skims through implant procedure and recovery logs, and comes upon clinical assessments. Gabriel reads page after page of his regularly-scheduled visits to his specialist, every three months since he was twelve, pausing at notable lines in the shorthand.

Subject exhibits rare predisposition to adaptability in physical and cognitive function, which undoubtedly lends itself to his accelerated integration of implant . . . Ability to decipher pattern is astounding, comprehension of shape and motion, and the relation ⸍ of the two, is intricate, complex, significant . . . Emotionally and socially withdrawn . . . Exacerbation by implant, probable. Acceleration and escalation, probable. Mental lapse, probable . . . Junior Science Subject 23 has proven to be valuable. Further study . . .

He rests his fingertips behind his ear, reaching for the spot deep inside his head where he often felt a foreign presence send shockwaves of impulse through him. He sought, and sought, and found, and is now left with decision. Gabriel can only feel nothing, though, once done digesting the information.

He has sat all day ingesting file upon file of protocol, test subjects, implicit and explicit crimes against science, humanity, decency. How far reaching it actually was, he could not have imagined. He finds the reason for it in the "Mission Statement" of Project CoEvoDevo. This file, he reopens without knowing. The title page is barren, except for the name CoEvoDevo, in large, bold, block lettering. Past numerous tables of content, an introduction comes. "Since the dawn of Man," it began, and continued as flowery and magniloquent, expounding on the nature of man, evolution, existence. The first line of substance comes two pages in:

The purpose of CoEvoDevo is the integration, not of Man and Science, or Technology, but, the application of Science to integrate Man and Information, so as to allow a fuller understanding of existence, inevitably spurring a necessary evolutionary period in accordance with Man's timeline.

His eyes scan the sentence until he is no longer reading, but merely gazing. His brain feels like it has expanded beyond its limit. It throbs as it seeks release from containment. The pain is oppressive. When he finally looks away, he veers from barren to hollow. He cannot contemplate the decisions before him. His inevitability is all he sees.

Gabriel goes to his bed, lifts the top mattress, and grabs a clear plastic bag filled with blue pills that was hidden there. He walks into the bathroom, turns on the tub faucet and gauges the temperature. He sits on the edge of the tub in the tiny bathroom of the small apartment, and waits for the tub to fill. The walls are painted a coarse pink, the sink is light blue. The tiles are cracked underneath his feet, tan tiles in tiny square sections that were once probably off-white. He turns off the faucet, making sure the water won't overflow, then gets in fully clothed. Gabriel anchors his feet against the wall and lets his body sink, keeping only his arms and face above water level. He closes his eyes. Gabriel wanted to be true to his pseudonym. He sought to be Anonymous.

"Love you, Ma," he says aloud.

Fourteen

The engineer stands on the balmy day, allowing the humidity to work his pores. He is dripping, drenched in sweat on the hazy day that's devoid of relief from wind. He had stayed in the camp for twenty-nine days after seven uneventful nights with the doctor, who was no longer able to house him. After which, he was not left with a host of choices.

He refused the hospital. He refused to deal with any faction of an establishment. He refused any option that would require him to renounce any co-conspirator, or discredit his recent experience, because he could not recall an experience that made him feel closer to reality. Nor could he accept the doctor's offer for safe passage off island, at least not yet. He did not feel whole, rational, or capable of a solitary existence, let alone one as a fugitive.

It was the camp; the transient camp was the only option he would accept. He felt an affinity for the place, and the doctor, although puzzled by the suggestion, assured him that since the criminal threat had been expunged, the camp would be safe. Yes, he would have to deal with patrols and occasional searches, but he would not be seen as a threat.

Now, standing outside his shanty tent, he begins to re-evaluate the idea. The shanty is actually more organized than he had imagined—food expeditions, thermal distillation sessions, clothing herders, rations; all the basics were collectively taken care of. There were those, he soon came to realize, who were much like him. Outbursts were frequent, even though silence was default. He would walk about and encounter the same lost eyes he imagined he also possessed. Still, there was a collectivity that endured, and a solemn tranquility that gave him solace. It served to temper him for some time, every day pacing him, relieving him of tension, absolving him from decision. But today, waking, and stepping out of the once-abandoned tent that he had claimed and made his shelter, something festers inside him, something he can neither shake nor imagine moving from. He starts walking down the shanty road, leaving his new life behind him.

One foot in front of the other is how he continues for a seemingly endless stretch of time, making sure to go toward more populated areas. Like a moth to a flame, he seeks civilization unremittingly, fluttering here and there, looking for a path, any route to his destination. He turns onto a street dotted with shops.

"The bus," he asks a pedestrian, in a weak voice. The words feel foreign and practically crumble in his mouth. He receives a strange look, and a finger pointed up the road, a direction he follows until he comes across a single metal pole, on which a screen enclosed in a hard clear case hosts the transit schedule.

The casing has been tampered with but remains uncompromised. Above the schedule, programming

155

transitions from weather, to news, to promotion, all subtitled and seamless. He focuses past the scratches and scrapes on the case; forty-five minutes is his expected wait. Having made sure to ask for change all along the way, a little past noon he boards the bus headed downtown with two dollars and seventy-three cents, twenty-three cents over the fare, which he tips the driver as he spills it all into the slot.

The bus driver gives him the once over, passengers stare. He passes by a mother with a child sitting in her lap. Other children who look related are scattered about the seats, and chatter with the child and amongst each other. He meanders to the back where he plops down into one of the few seats available on the crowded bus, next to a man holding an open liquor bottle. He sits, and fits in with the somber crowd.

Staring out the window, decay and disarray stream by him. Uncertain faces drift through the streets, searching for something he can't imagine. The bus stops and the sole individual there makes no attempt to move; instead, he sits on a bench with a vacant stare, holding an open can. The bob of his head is barely perceptible.

The bus continues down a stretch of dilapidated housing and neglected communities that range from urban to rural, until it takes a sharp left where the scenery abruptly transitions. For half an hour, he watches as walks become more trim and kempt, and houses become larger, until they become buildings. Downtown, he gets off the bus.

Modern facades and domes surround him, the architecture overpowering the landscape. Only alert faces instinctively navigate the district, their imploring eyes prove enough to make him uncomfortable. He immediately looks down at his worn clothing, and quickly strokes his disheveled facial hair.

In the distance, towering over all other buildings, is his destination. He walks through the maze of buildings, wildly glancing back at unfriendly looks until he begins to ascend the steps to the Academy of Sciences.

Inside, he rotates, taking in the grand lobby. He looks at the poster to his side. Fireworks explode on the large poster, calling for patrons to help celebrate the birthday of the 'Resident Spirit Bear.'

"Can I help you?" asks the receptionist.

"Uh, yeah. I, uh . . . " he mumbles, completely caught off guard.

"Excuse me?   Are you here to see the new quantum computation exhibit?" she asks, looking to his beard.

"Uh, no. No. I would, uh, like to see the CEO of LE," he spouts out as he approaches her.

She leans back and immediately looks less amiable. "What would make you think they would be here, sir?"

"I know her main office is here."

The receptionist looks at him concernedly. "Do you have an—actually, I'm going to have to ask you to leave," she responds.

"No, I . . . uh, I—"

"I've already asked you to leave, sir. Please. I'd rather this not go too far. You have ten seconds to go before I—"

"No, no, tell her, tell her CoEvoDevo. Tell her CoEvoDevo is here to see her."

"I don't have time—"

"Tell her. She'll know. Tell her. You'll be making a mistake if you don't."

The confidence in his voice stalls her. She continues evaluating him. Slowly, she picks up a cordless phone and presses a single button. Her words are inaudible to him, and she never looks away. Two individuals with cameras in tote and a general affable nature stroll in the main entrance and approach the receptionist, only to receive a single, raised, index finger. Again, she speaks into the phone, and then drops it.

"Just one moment, someone will be down to pick you up shortly. Please take a seat, sir." she informs, with her eyes now cutting into him.

He sits on the large, long, Koa bench on the wall opposite of her, and continues to look around the lobby. A strange bewilderment is present in his expression, something that draws the receptionist's attention even while assisting the others.

"Richard Wright?" the engineer hears from a large stout man in a black suit who ambles toward him.

"Yes," the engineer's low voice is hoarse.

"Please come this way." The man directs, forcing the engineer to keep pace. They turn right, and then left, and to the left are a row of elevators. The security officer places his keycard to the terminal and it beeps. Seconds later, the elevator doors open. Inside, he places his keycard to a terminal, and another beep sounds. He presses several of the elevator buttons in succession, none of which remain lit. The elevator ascends. The engineer tries to maintain composure, glancing only once at the security guard, who looks stoically ahead with his arms folded before him. His sunglasses shield any emotion.

The elevator stops and all the floor lights on the elevator panel illuminate. The door opens to reveal a capacious room and a walkway flanked on both sides by antiques and adornments. At the end of the long walkway is a single desk, from behind which, a voice calls to him. "Mr. Wright, welcome. Please, come take a seat."

He looks to the security officer to his left, and then, alone, he steps off the elevator carriage and onto the dark tile. Walking toward the desk, he notices a seemingly life-sized, ivory elephant sculpture to his right. Further down the phantasmagoric stretch, he sees a huge spinning globe, on which news stories randomly sprout from red dots in regions of the world.

"You seem fascinated," says the woman behind the desk. He looks ahead, and walks forward, without diverting attention. He approaches and stops behind one of the two arm chairs before the desk.

"Welcome to my sanctuary, Mr. Wright. This is where I spend most of my time. Please, have a seat."

He looks at her, unable to decipher a background. Her dark brown skin is smooth, beautiful, he thinks. Her face is aged, but still pretty, with long lashes attached to the lids that house her light brown eyes. Her shoulder length hair is silken, and she appears small but sturdy. He sits to her right.

"What was it you wanted to see me about, Mr. Wright? How can I help you?"

"Is that elephant really ivory?"

She smiles. "Yes, but not from any animal. Synthetic,

amazing actually, in my opinion . . . An interesting question, but I'm sure it's not what you came here for," she finishes, while tucking her hand under her chin and leaning on her left armrest.

"I know about you."

"What exactly do you know about me, Mr. Wright?"

"I know about CoEvoDevo, about the experiments, about everything."

"Alright," she says, righting herself.

" . . . Alright—that's it?"

"Is there something I should do, Mr. Wright?"

"Shouldn't you be worried about what I'm going to do?"

"If you truly believe there is something, do your best—or your worst seems more suitable for many reasons. Not to be rude, but I'm very busy. Maybe we should start with what you want. Do you know what you want, Mr. Wright?"

" . . . I want to know why, why all the experimentation, why go this far? LE can't be hurting, you run an island. Is it the government, a product—"

"There, there, Mr. Wright. I guess that mind of yours is still working. It is a product, Mr. Wright, but not just any product; it is the product of man's history, the result of years of evolutionary history. Can you imagine no longer having to be beholden to time, money, cultural restraints, society, external detriments? Can you imagine being able to download and integrate information just like that?" The snap of her fingers resounds throughout the cavernous room.

"What are you talking about?"

"The 'largest outdoor mall in the world,' how profitable do you think it is?"

"I don't know. Very, I can imagine," the engineer answers combatively.

"I think you'd be interested to know that the profits are negligible. Actually, with the fanfare and all the backroom wheeling and dealing, some quarters it's in the red. Not by very much, and, of course, the books don't show, but sometimes a bit in the red." She chuckles. "Now, why do you think it would still be open and running?"

"I don't know. What the fuck does this have to do with anything? Maybe you thought it would work. Maybe it's for all those backroom deals. Why don't you just tell me?" the engineer asks, visibly agitated.

She pauses after the outburst. ". . . The twenty-fourth of February was the day of the groundbreaking, the twenty-fourth of February was also the day of the ribbon cutting. The twenty-fourth of February is the birthday of the founder of this company. Naturally, it had a different name then. That mall is a monument. Men used to build monuments out of admiration, adoration, reverence. Now, money makes money, and lauds those who conceived the possibility by building them money pits.

"This, Mr. Wright, is indicative of the time we live in—it's the corporate way. At some point, we decided, and never amended the decision, that corporations were people. People I know, when they eat they get full; they get to a certain height, they stop growing. But corporations, they only know how to grow, without limit. They never stop, never satisfied, never fulfilled. The bottom line is always more. The culture wars destroy society and the corporations run the world. It is time for man to evolve."

"How can you . . . you're CEO of the largest fucking corporation in the world, and you've stepped on every human rights and ethics code imaginable. What gives you the right to talk like this? You can't see the hypocrisy?"

"I was born, Mr. Wright, in India. My father, also born there, was an international mutt. He was a travelling doctor, the sort that's recognized by international institutions but also discreetly takes money from drug dealers to 'save the world.' You know, an idealist. One night--I can only imagine a lonely, smog-filled night--he raped a very beautiful and very poor woman. A truth I only learned well into adulthood. The Pacific Islands, to Japan, Hawaii, and all over Europe, contributed genetics to the rare beauty and insanity that was my mother. I have no idea why my mother was even there, and I can only imagine the karma threads that intertwined them, but can you imagine what I went through under India's neo-caste system as a product of the union? I was stripped from her at birth—a hidden blessing—and was bound to live by a social contract I signed before I even knew how to write. And now I am the CEO of the 'largest fucking corporation in the world,' as you so eloquently articulated. I have never had the comfort of innocence, let alone the ability to indulge in it. Change, in my experience, comes along with extremely hard work and enduring compromise, primarily with yourself.

"I did not ask for this current situation, Mr. Wright. I inherited it. When I became CEO of this institution, my job was to manage and mitigate for a probable transition. The former, defunct CEO had lost the trust of the board. The company was stagnant, as it was when the founder died before it metamorphosed. He promised results, and we found out too

162

late how committed he was to that promise when we discovered his perversions of science. In pursuit of a Holy Grail or Eureka, he committed all manner of atrocities.

"He unsuccessfully tried to destroy the evidence before we caught him, and left us with a rather prodigious quandary. Of course, it was to be resolved in-house, but what of the ongoing actualities? It wasn't until we dissected these cases that we discovered real applications for these experiments. He was a monster, but as far as R&D is concerned, he was godsend. We continued a select few, put an end his regime and hung his picture somewhere in memoriam."

"So you're absolved of all wrongdoing? You hide behind the monster and continue his work, all while raking in dollars?"

A yawn accentuates her fatigue. "I cannot speak for another, Mr. Wright, but I know I am a monster. Was it not the devil, by which, being cast into the pit of hell, illuminated the true path to the Lord? I believe in capital, or currency transaction. I very rarely use paper money. The acquisition of material holds little weight with me. I have convinced others of a certain path, one that is truly in my heart. I cannot speak of their intention, nor will I deny any manipulation of them."

"What are you even saying?" the engineer asks as he buries his head deep in his palms.

"What I'm saying is that we have advanced well beyond what the average man can fathom, well beyond screens and hybrids. But where do we see the application? In luxury, where we build an abundance of nothing? In aggression, where one man creates a weapon to alleviate his fear of another, whom he will cyclically teach to fear him? In bureaucracy, where paranoia safeguards power? We are

163

stuck at combustion because of our resource addiction. Patent law continues to stifle creativity. Synthesis threatens all—"

"Look at your goddamn elephant!" the engineer blurts, now rolling his head in his palms.

"I do, every time I step into this office. At the start of the millennia, we grew a billion in a decade, a short time after which, there's been a steady decline. Do you think this is coincidental, Mr. Wright? By the end of these ten years, we will be down a billion. Automation will take more jobs, and bureaucracy will support less until a happy median is reached. What about the mean, Mr. Wright? This is the next step in evolution, CoEvoDevo. Everyone will have access to information. Just a simple download and it will be stored in your brain. Country codes, background, discrimination, superfluous constructs will no longer be pertinent to individual development; only creativity, productivity, truly individual interaction with the world will soon be achieved. Manufactured stratification will become obsolete. We are approaching a true meritocracy."

"And me? Am I in one of these databases? I wasn't in any of the files; am I a subject?"

"Yes, Mr. Wright, as you've probably deduced, you are. Since your "incident" brought you to our attention, you've been looked into. You're undoubtedly a product of the Docupurge. A small amount of your records have been recovered, and your records off-island have been very carefully tampered with. Yes, like your friend Mike"—the engineer raises his head—"we believe your memory has been altered. But, unlike him, we believe you suffered from some medical condition. It was a project of his, taking criminals and the mentally impaired and

164

trying to rehabilitate them."

"How could you do this?"

"Honestly, it's doubtful you can. There are parts of your brain used primarily for memory, and certain types of it, but it truly is a process that requires the entire grey matter. In essence, his method was to mute your previous person all the way down to zero, and then replace it with a person that they turn up to, say, volume ten. Definitely a discontinued project, in my opinion, bad science in general. On top of that, you've been downloaded with advanced mechanical engineering. You have a criminal background. You were a career criminal, in fact, violent crime, petty theft, et cetera. And from your behavioral and cognitive assessments, I suspect that—because of your former, socio-economic background—you harbor an undiagnosed mental disorder as well. Schizophrenia is probable. I'm not sure to what extent that was known.

"What you must understand is that the problem was not in the theory, but the application. If you consider your brain as hardware, which it is, everything it takes in is software, environment, education, all software. This is the convergence of nature and nurture, Mr. Wright. My former counterpart rushed. In essence, he forced input. The result, as you have undoubtedly witnessed, is jarring.

"The hardware-software bond within humans is very significant. It produces an individual persona and anima naturally. Issues arise with competing input, the individual begins to split; the mind shatters. Now, with proper mapping of your hardware infrastructure, particularly the medial temporal region, we can safely input. To get a bit more complex, it became a matter of synchronization versus syncopation. The latter, we discovered to be less obtrusive."

"And Charles?" the engineer asks somberly.

"I thought you would want to see your friend. He is here, safe with us. I did you the service of sending for him. He is currently waiting in the lobby behind us. Would you like to see him?"

"Yes," he says weakly.

"Marissa, please send in Mr. Charles," the CEO says into her intercom.

"Yes, right away."

The CEO points to a door to her right. The engineer stares to his left. The knob turns, and Commander Charles appears, completely unscathed and dressed in a grey suit. He walks behind the CEO, and stands to her right.

"Good to see you, Rich," Charles greets, clasping his hands before him.

"Charles," the engineer whispers in disbelief.

"Your friend, as you can see, is safe with us," the CEO reassures. "He actually is a remarkable man, and specimen. We have high hopes for him within our institution."

"What are you talking about? Did you brainwash him?"

The CEO can't control her laughter. "Free will, Mr. Wright, true free will is my ultimate goal. Besides, I cannot trust anyone, and therefore work with them, if they are not in control of their own faculties and decision-making. Honestly, I wonder if it would even work on him. On the contrary, we stripped him of his falsehood, reawakened him."

"What reawakening?"

"As you're probably aware, Mr. Charles here was a super-soldier of sorts, the kind without the superpowers, of course.

166

He, like you, was not in the files you were gifted. But he is a test subject. He underwent memory augmentation similar to yours, as well as logic and logistics downloads. He was in a coma when he was found by the prior administration. He was brought home after a severe service injury, an explosion that threw him a good distance, I believe."

"Wait, you said 'gifted.' Files we were gifted? What are you talking about?"

"Do you truly believe we would allow that much data to be taken from us? Everything in turn, Mr. Wright. When he emerged from his coma, his significant other at the time rushed to the hospital to see him. Was rushing, I should say. She, herself, was involved in an accident."

"After being informed of her death, the next morning, Mr. Charles once again slipped into a coma." Charles' head hangs so low that his eyes are not visible. "We had, I'd say, partnerships, with hospitals, private prisons. Veterans, like the homeless and the incarcerated, were a large number of the test subjects, which is why they are disparately . . . people of color," she laughs. "None of us know how to describe race anymore, huh? His background was impressive. He was an orphan and overwhelmingly discreet, which made everything easier, not much in his history to clean up. But it was the last piece that touched the researchers and also touched me when I discovered it. His was an experiment maybe of the soul, something metaphysical, for sure. An unexplained coma, could they wake him up after expunging the bad parts?

"His memory was altered, *that* memory was altered, and he woke up. After releasing him from the prison that was built in his mind, I can understand why. He's a sincere man, and his is a grief few will feel." Charles' head remains lowered. "Suggestive ideas were planted in his mind; they predisposed him to this island, and this company, and undoubtedly assisted in bringing him here. But through it all, he refused to let go, to let her go. Isn't that why we're all here?"

As far as those files, they were given to you. The whole operation was an inside job."

"How is that possible? It was only us, the Doc . . ."

"The doctor is one of the brightest minds we've ever employed, with enough demons in his past now to challenge that seat in hell. We kept him on after the transition, but he began to unwind. He was getting bad, thin, distant. Insanity, undoubtedly, had taken root. There was a mutual agreement that lab work no longer suited him. At the time, Anon was on the rise and we needed an ally in their ranks. He had an affinity for technology, and a healthy programming background. He agreed as long as he still had privileges and involvement in the work. Quite frankly, I dare say he's very good at his new line of work, and I must say he seems to be enjoying himself and his new life as a secret agent of sorts," she smiles.

"So, you're Anon."

"By no means, Mr. Wright, but they're definitely people of interest. They're actually a sophisticated organization, with integrated yet independent cell structure. Our doctor, after years of disseminating all manner of information, still only has a certain level of trust. We hoped to change that with this leak. Theirs is a platform I'm intrigued by."

"So you incriminated yourself just so you can get closer to a hacker collective? How does that make sense?" the engineer cries, unable to hide his exasperation.

"Incriminate? How so? We hope to gain vital publicity with the leak and all the conspiracy theorizing it will conjure. Our project launch is impending. Who but the most hardcore skeptics believe anti-establishment rhetoric, even when all signs point to its truth? It'll be chalked up to competitive banter and attempted sabotage, something else we can use against Mr. Nuong and Invision. Can you believe they would sully a contract with us with a wide-scale espionage plan? Everyone spies, but to attempt to infiltrate," she says, shaking her head.

"So Nuong was part of this?"

"Of course, along with that bit of rubbish you know as Jim that I'm ashamed to say once worked for this company. Never shy away from war, Mr. Wright. You just have to ensure the politics are right."

"You can't believe this won't be exploited."

"I believe this is evolution, Mr. Wright. A vital stimulus has been introduced. Whether it is natural selection, mutation, genetic or even social drift, Man will change. And I'm confident it will be for the better.

"Alright then," she says as she claps her hands together," it was an amazing chat, but I do need to get back to work. I thought you deserved some answers after coming all this way, but I can't afford to be so generous with my time any longer," she says, pressing a button on her intercom.

"I don't care if you kill me! You're insane." the engineer yells. "I'm going to let someone know. I'm going to let everyone know!"

"No. You won't," she dictates. "You're taking a trip today, Mr. Wright. We indulged the Doctor. He wanted some days to study your behavior, compare statistics, and then we gave you the chance to live autonomously based on his recommendation. It was not an easy concession. You left the camp. Clearly a discontentment exists within you. It will grow. You are a clear risk to yourself and others, and will be decommissioned."

"Decommissioned?" the engineer asks, looking again to Charles, who only stares back.

"Yes, Mr. Wright. Have you felt faulty, uncontrollable, estranged from self? Have you been of much use to anyone, to yourself even? Of course we will do extensive testing on you, but I can't imagine we will find much different than what I presume now. The problem is that there is no fix. Your mind was not strong enough for any input, and will be unable to piece together output. It will shatter. You are a product of the Docupurge, so we cannot even know the full extent of your augmentation. Decommissioning is best. In essence, you will be lobotomized, conditioned, and sent to the Farm, where you will have quite a peaceful, and I would say, enjoyable, existence. It is a process that we have been undergoing slowly, as we could not recall all of you at once. Your decommissioning has simply been moved up. I recommend the Mac Nut Farm; the most positive assessments come from there. You will make your own choice, of course."

"And Mike?" he says, trying to find some hint, some message, as he looks again to him.

"Mr. Charles has actually proven sympathetic to our cause. Once the agenda was explained, he understood. I do believe there was a Commander Jezequel who was involved in all manner of terrorist activity, and recruited officers to quiet

Commander Charles after he learned of those activities. He simply defended himself. He will soon be exonerated of all wrongdoing and commended for his work. It's a shame he was framed, and had to become a fugitive to clear his name. People enjoy hero stories; I think they will particularly like this snippet when they read the news. We have given him a choice, and he has pledged his service. He has a place now with us." The elevators open. Two, large security personnel, walk formally toward them. "Here, we look even past quality, on to value. He is a valuable asset, who has already, and I'm sure will continue to prove his value."

"You brainwashed him!"

"I assure you we did not. Like me, he is someone who has seen the cruelty and potential the world possesses. He simply believes in evolution."

The engineer looks back and sees the men nearly behind him. Once more, he looks to Charles. Feverish now, he looks for any sign. Charles peers at the engineer and clenches his jaw. The engineer lunges forward, and grabs a pen from the desk. Charles simultaneously lunges toward the CEO. The engineer, now armed, hops the desk and dives straight at the CEO. The two guards reach for their hips. Charles leaps into the air. He collides with the engineer. They roll off the edge of the desk and Charles tackles the engineer to the ground. Charles holds the engineer under him until security secures him.

The guards hold the engineer up as he frantically shakes his head. "How the fuck could you! How the fuck could you! How the fuck could you? How the fuck could you?" he continues, until the question becomes a silent whimper.

"I worked under AfriComm once," Charles begins to speak, as he stands. "There was a conflict. There were never wars on that continent, only conflicts. I guess the context doesn't matter. One day, me and a small group, we're trekking on this back road through the brush, staying alert, and in the distance there's this wall in the middle of the road. Takes me a second to realize what it is, still I didn't believe. Not until we got closer, and you see these hands, and legs, and eyes.

"There were bodies burnt, not charred, not unrecognizable, just burnt. Before or after life, who knows? Wall has to be at least five feet, maybe ten wide. To the left, toward the bottom, is a little girl. It made no sense; she still had some hair. I couldn't help it, just cried, bawled, right there. The media, never a word. Our intelligence says it's local atrocities, they say it's us, someone blames neighboring tribes, terrorists. Maybe someone ties it to oil, the price of tea in China. Who cares, right? But me, all I could think of was that little girl with the hair. I never forget. I never can.

"The image, it played in my head sometimes. Sometimes, it was just a feeling; if that even makes sense. She was something else they took from me, and something else that lingered, even after the memory was erased. Something needs to change, in us, not outside. Inside."

The engineer continues to shake his head after exhausting himself of the same question while Charles looks on. "You know where to find me," Charles says to the CEO, before leaving the room.

"You know what is stronger in humans than even survival?" the CEO asks rhetorically. "Ideas. Shared ideas create the strongest bonds imaginable. Thank you for your sacrifice, Mr.

Wright. Please, escort Mr. Wright to R&D. They'll know what to do with him."

Fifteen

"Alicia! You watching that TV? You finish your homework!"

"Yes, Mom!"

"Did you finish your dishes? You know it's your turn."

"Yes, Mom. They're done."

"You sure you finished your homework?" her mother asks, as she appears behind her and leans over the sofa back.

"Yeah, Mom. I'm all done."

"Alright," she says, kissing her cheek before walking away.

"You know you didn't finish your homework."

"Shut up, Bobby."

"You really ought to finish your homework."

"Shut up, Bobby."

"I'm just say—"

"SHHH SHHHHH, I wanna hear this."

". . . The Evo chip. A new development from LE now streamlines information directly to your mind. The wireless Evo chip can sync with your personal brainwaves, and deliver information directly to you—"

"O-M-G! I want one of those," Alicia gushes.

"Cooooollllllll."

174

"Shut up, Bobby. Can you imagine not having to remember anything anymore?"

"Cooooolllllll."

"You're such an idiot."

". . . online to learn more about this revolutionary technology. LE, Live Experience."

"Man, whoever doesn't have one of those . . . It's going to really suck not having one of those."

"You'll still suck after you get one."

"Just shut up, Bobby!"

Charles sits before the oak desk in his office. He holds a manila folder and leafs through the pages. Eventually, he lays it down and walks to the window to view the lush foliage outside, allowing himself to get lost.

He returns to his desk and opens the top drawer. Reaching in, he takes out a framed picture. Her dark hair, her olive skin, the picture that he found online was one he had taken himself. "Emille," he says out loud, conjuring a memory that felt lost for too long, and trying to imprint the name in his mind. He couldn't shake the recent foreboding of losing her, among other things, again. He traces her jaw and her face with his finger. Carefully, he returns the picture frame, and then picks up another.

Gwen is smiling; her dimples indent her face. It was another picture he took, on her birthday. She leans over a cake as smoke rises from the candles. It was just the two of them that year, he recalls. She told him later that it was the best birthday she ever had. "I'm sorry," he says, "I promise."

He places the picture on the desk and answers the intercom. "Yes?" he says.

"Commissioner, your 2:30 appointment . . ."

Richard holds a Mac Nut and peers at the shell through the split husk.   His thumb caresses the outer husk, enjoying the texture that reminds him so much of a pecan.   Slowly, he reaches his index finger inside, running it along the chocolate brown inner flesh of the husk, then moving it to the dark brown shell.   So enraptured, he inadvertently dislodges the husk which falls to the ground unnoticed.

Looking down at the macadamia nut, the contours give him pleasure and he smiles.   He looks to a Macadamia Nut Tree. Something intangible, something beyond its simple beauty, gives him pleasure, so he smiles.   He looks to those around him, the group, the camaraderie, something gives him pleasure; he smiles.   A warm breeze wisps by his face. The sensations, the Farm, everything gives him pleasure.   He smiles. The only thing he thinks will give him more pleasure is work. He smiles and continues.